The Indelible Heart

Marianne K. Martin

T0161497

Bywater Books

Ann Arbor

Bywater Books

Bywater Books First Edition: July 2011

Printed in the United States of America
on acid-free paper.

Cover designer: Bonnie Liss (Phoenix Graphics)

Bywater Books
PO Box 3671
Ann Arbor Mi 48106-3671
www.bywaterbooks.com

ISBN: 978-1-932859-77-5

This novel is a work of fiction. Although parts of the plot
were inspired by actual events, all characters and events
described by the author are fictitious. No resemblance
to real persons, dead or alive, is intended.

Mixed Sources
Product group from well-managed
forests and other controlled sources
www.fsc.org Cert no. SW-COC-002283
© 1996 Forest Stewardship Council
FSC

Dedication

This story deals with loss, surviving it and thriving in spite of it. As losses touched my real life, taking these characters emotionally where they needed to go became a test of will. It took a long time, but those I've lost would not have allowed me to give up or give in.

It is with a heavy, but thankful heart, that I acknowledge the impact of these special women on my life and dedicate this work to them:

As the oldest child in our family, I was not born with a natural big sister—that special person, a little older, a lot wiser, to share dreams and secrets and family time with. So, Jean became that for me. Her smile made me happy, her singing voice gave me goose bumps, and the magic she worked teaching children inspired me. I trusted her and loved her as my very own.

During a pivotal time in my life when I needed validation and encouragement to be who I thought I was, Joyce stepped in. With few words, and actions that spoke volumes, she was there every day—letting me be who I was, empowering and demanding and not letting me settle for less than my best. She showed me who I was, and I believed her.

And I was blessed in my life with one of those rare larger than life women whose talents and achievements touched so many lives. Barb read between and saw beyond. She said that I dropped them like pearls, those singular truths in my stories, and let them roll along quietly. She found every one. Her laugh was contagious, her support and love immeasurable. She made me strive always to be my best and was there to notice when I was. I admired her and loved her, and I miss her more than I can say.

Acknowledgments

Although it may seem so at times, writers never do this alone. We wrestle the words to our stories, our thoughts and our emotions, onto the page as life continues to evolve around us. And there are times, as with this book, that this writer appreciates more than ever the support and love of family and friends.

My sister, Trish, is at the other end of the phone day or night, always there to share the sadness and the tears, the love and the laughter. She knows how much it means.

Also, there every day, believing in me and making it possible for me to do what I do, is my partner, Jo. She knew what I should do before I did, believed in the possibility when I didn't.

And, just as appreciated is the support and patience of Kelly Smith of Bywater Books, business partner, editor, and friend, who gave me the time, without added pressure, to work through some rough times and finish this book.

Finally, I am a writer blessed and thankful to be a part of Bywater Books. I cannot thank Val McDermid enough for what she does for this company, and I could not have a more gifted editor than Kelly Smith. Together with copy editor Caroline Curtis, graphic artist Bonnie Liss, and publicity agent Michele Karlsberg, I could not have a better team to work with.

Foreword

On May 5, 1992 my mother Susan Pittmann and her lesbian partner Christine Puckett were murdered by their neighbor James Brooks. Newspapers in Detroit and Huron Township, Michigan reported that the double homicide was the culmination of an ongoing battle over property lines. My mother was fifty-five, healthy and vibrant with positive ideas about the future. Christine was thirty-nine, energetic and busy raising her teenage son. Brooks was slow to reflect and quick to anger. He became enraged when he saw my mother and Christine publicly expressing affection. By erecting a privacy fence between these two rural properties, Mom and Christine intended to bring a peaceful resolution to Brooks' complaints. However, it became clear that he was enraged about their gay relationship, and that not seeing them together was not enough. He vigorously complained to neighbors where he found support for his rage, and he formulated his murder plan.

From police reports, it's clear that he shot Christine first from the side door of his house and then as he walked over to view her body that was face-down in the grass, he lifted his gun and shot her in the back. I imagine that just before he pulled the trigger, he thought the words which he told the police later, "It had to be done". My mother was on the kitchen phone with the emergency operator, reporting that Brooks had threatened their lives when Christine was first shot. She immediately dropped the telephone, ran outside, and stood in front of Brooks, weaponless. I imagine she asked him why he did it, and in answer, he shot her just below the heart.

Brooks' determined discriminatory attitude has troubled me ever since. How did he become so certain about his decision to murder my mother and Christine? After the deaths, I watched in astonishment as the actual motivation for the crime was determined to be a property dispute instead of a hate crime. Newspapers reported exaggerated stories casting my mother and Christine in a harsh light, which apparently had nothing to do with their sexual preference. I was shocked to see my mother, a dynamic loving people-person characterized as a temperamental abuser of animals while Brooks was portrayed as an elderly man who was pushed to the limits of tolerance by his unreasonable neighbors. Neighbors reported that he was upset about my mother's pit bull trespassing onto his property. No one explained that my mother's dog, Ms. Pitt, was an elderly, overweight, exhausted, and non-territorial dog that was given a daily dose of thyroid medication just to stay alert. No mention was made of her activism within the gay community, and that she and Christine were founding members of the Affirmations Gay and Lesbian Community Center in Downriver Detroit. No mention was made that she was a loving mother of five children and devoted grandmother to eight. No mention was made about how much we would continue to miss her for the rest of our lives.

After reading these news reports, I quickly understood that Brooks had not acted alone. In fact, it was a narrow-minded society that provided ammunition for this crime. Only the gay community stood strong and honestly told the truth about these murders. They loudly proclaimed that this double homicide was not a neighborhood feud but a hate crime. As a continued tribute to the gay community, I am honored at Marianne K. Martin's request to write the foreword of her latest novel, *The Indelible Heart*. This novel extends some of the plot threads related to my mother and Christine which appeared in Martin's first novel *Love in Balance* and succeeds in giving a personal face to the events surrounding the murders. Though it is a work of fiction, the narrative highlights how in fact, the gay community rallied together to fight homophobia and violence in response to this shocking crime. I encourage people to read this profoundly moving novel and realize that it is our duty as members of society to stand together and continue a united struggle against intolerance and violence.

Cynthia Pittmann
April 2011

Chapter One

"Over my fat, very dead carcass!"

The words sliced through settling drywall dust and blasted into the open house ahead of Sharon. "You can put that on my tombstone," she continued at the top of her voice.

Kasey rushed into the room to another blustering rage. "What, Sharon? What is it now?"

"This!" she shouted, throwing a tightly folded newspaper to the floor. "I swear to God, Kasey . . ."

Kasey frowned and turned her face from the rising plume of displaced dust as she reached to pick up the paper.

"I *will* kill him this time, Kase. I swear to God I will."

It took a moment to find it, but the small article at the bottom of the page was clearly the source of Sharon's rage.

GOVERNOR COMTEMPLATES RELEASE

Despite objections from LGBT organizations, including the NCLR, Equality Michigan, and The Gay & Lesbian Task Force, Governor Holmes is contemplating the early release from prison of Charles Crawford.

Crawford was convicted in 1999 of murdering Evonne Pearlman and Donna Corbett, a lesbian couple who lived next door to him. The women were shot in their front yard. Crawford is currently serving two life sentences, but was hospitalized recently due to ill health. "He's very sick," said Jeremy Crawford, his son and spokesman for the family. "We just want him to be able to die at home surrounded by his family."

"I don't care if he has two breaths left, he can take them in prison. He sure as hell didn't give Donna and Evonne any choice, did he? What's his son gonna say next, that Donna and Evonne got to die at home, so why shouldn't his father? How insane is that?"

"I can't imagine that the governor would grant this, Sharon. It's just the media not having anything else to talk about. It's a slow news day, so they start speculating, that's all."

"Hell, Kasey, it's been four weeks of *his* family, *his* illness, *his* need for mercy. I'm tired of it being about him. I'm tired of people pissin' all over what's right and fair."

Kasey tossed the paper on the floor near the door and grabbed Sharon's arm. "Come on, Sharon. There's one thing I've learned over the past few years, and that's that you can't just spew anger out there into a headwind. Take a walk with me."

Sharon turned obediently and with mission-like sharpness marched out the front door and down the sidewalk to the next driveway before Kasey caught up. One driveway passed, then the next, marking the boundaries between the wood-framed houses lining the street. A slideshow of sorts, passing by unnoticed, dotted with neatly groomed little yards, and foreclosure signs. Symbols in contradiction. One, a symbol of lives on track, modest and secure, the other of interrupted dreams and tough times, like the house the Hollander Davis Company was renovating.

"So are we marching our way to the governor's house?" Kasey asked, matching Sharon's hard, brisk pace as closely as she could.

"He's evil," Sharon said, her eyes set severely forward. "Pure evil. No righteous God would let him breathe even one more breath."

They continued walking, as if time was of the essence, as if reaching some unknown destination would be just in time to set right the injustice. "I don't like even the thought of the possibility, Sharon, any more than you do, but stressing like this isn't a solution. The organizations have it. We're not alone, it's not like before. We have clout now in numbers . . ."

Sharon heard Kasey's words, at least the sound of them, humming beside her like wide rubber tires on warm pavement—the meaning lost in a hypnotic cadence, but it didn't matter. The words, the walk, the purpose, were all too familiar. The years had offered up too many reasons for them, too many times. The deaths—Evonne and Donna's, her own brother Ronnie, and mother, Kasey's mother; the loves lost; the depression. Always, though, there was Kasey, true and constant. Always there. Always.

Their pace had slowed, purposeful still, but no longer possessed of some great mission. Sharon tapped a basketball with the side of her foot and sent it rolling off the sidewalk and back into a small front yard.

It worked, this mutual reliance they shared, as well as any therapy ever had.

Sharon's voice had tempered. "I didn't think I'd ever have to waste another thought on that monster. But here he is again."

"I'm sure no one else has given him much thought in years either."

Sharon nodded, pulling a wallet from her jeans pocket and flipping it open. "But, there's not a day that I don't think of *them*." The picture had been everyone's favorite of the two women—heads pressed together with cheeky smiles and arms wrapped around one another—the same one used in the obituary. She'd kept it there, in the front right next to Laura's. "I love these souls. Next to you and Laura . . ."

"I know, Sharon. I know how much they meant—to all of us. Please don't go there."

Sharon closed the wallet and shoved it back into her pocket. As the tears welled, she clenched the muscles of her jaw into rigid knots. "*Mean*, Kasey, how much they mean. Don't drop them off into obscurity." A quick swipe with the back of her hand eliminated a tear before it could make it to her cheek. "We can't let them make this about him—"

"All right, all right, that's not what I was saying. You know how I feel. I just don't want you going down that emotional hole. Okay?"

Sharon turned to start back toward the house. A half a block later she said quietly, "We're crawlin', Kase. It's been three months since the House vote. The Senate votes aren't there to pass the Hate Crimes Bill. It's gonna die again. All these years of letters and petitions and beatings and death, and where the hell are we?"

"It's going to be all right, Sharon. It's not like before, we've made tremendous progress. We have a political voice—strong organizations that have the media's ear. Look at the connections and communications online—raising awareness, raising money. All of that has identified it, and named it. It's a crime now, it's a hate crime . . . It'll be okay, Sharon."

"It'll never be okay."

Chapter Two

He should be dead. Or dying—alone, crying out for someone to take his hand, to tenderly touch his brow, to care. But no one should be there, no one should care. He needs to die alone, desperate, suffering in pain that only death can relieve.

Sharon visualized his face, creased hatred morphing into lonely desperation. Greasy beads of fear, pleading eyes. *Will he actually pray to God at the end? Ask for forgiveness he didn't deserve? No one that evil would, could. Or will he go to his grave believing in his own perverted righteousness?*

"Hey." Kim leaned over the back of the couch and wrapped her arms around Sharon's shoulders. "Come on, it's a good paintball night, all women."

"I don't want to go. You go ahead if you want."

"Come on. You've been in some kind of a funk ever since I got here. You need to get out and do something." She circled the end of the couch and sat folded onto her knees next to Sharon.

Normally there was no resisting Kim's youthful exuberance, no matter how long the workday or how painful her knees, but tonight youth and exuberance wasn't enough. "Just the thought of any kinda gun in my hands is really too much tonight."

"Are you still thinking about that old man? He's paid. He's dying. He'll probably go straight to hell if there is such a thing. Let it go, Sharon."

"Sometimes I wish I could. But other times—what happens if we let too many things go? What kind of message does that send?"

Kim's brow pressed into a rare frown. "We? There's a 'they' out there, you know. Lots of organizations who are watch-doggin' for us. You take things way too personally."

"This *is* personal. Can you name them—those organizations that are doin' all the watch-doggin'?"

"Yes," came the distinctively indignant reply. "I can. NCLR," she pressed her face just a shade closer, "HRC—"

"All right, all right."

"Like I said, lots."

"And how do you suppose all those organizations keep doing what they do?" Sharon watched Kim do exactly as expected—shut down and get up from the couch. Her tone became less accusatory. "Because a lot of people are taking things personally, Kim, that's all I'm trying to say."

"Yeah, I get it," she said, retrieving her jacket from the back of a chair. "You don't have to educate me."

"Wait, Kim." Sharon hurried to her side. "I'm sorry. I didn't mean for it to sound like that."

"How else could it sound?"

"It *could* sound like I wasn't an asshole if," Sharon wrapped her arms around a hesitant Kim, "I wasn't an asshole." So thin, so small, turning in her arms, facing her, forgiving her. "Don't go yet, okay? I promise not to go all negative on you again."

"Maybe we could go to the bar tonight, get your mind off it."

Sharon pressed her cheek to the youthful tousle of strawberry blond hair. "Can we stay here? Maybe watch a movie?"

"I guess. As long as it isn't Chevy Chase again. I don't know how you can still laugh after you've seen the same stupid movie a hundred times."

"It's the same thing as looking at a beautiful woman for the umpteenth time. She's still beautiful. It's a visual thing. The same way people like to watch some moron try to skateboard down a railing. They watch it over and over, knowing that the skateboard is going to fly out and the guy is going to ride the rest of the rail on his gonads."

"Once is enough for me," she replied with a cocked grin and a step from Sharon's embrace. "Well, if I can't get you out of here, at least I'm picking the movie."

Sharon watched Kim, kneeling and sorting through the DVDs, gathering snacks from the kitchen, settling beside her on the couch. *From Day One she seemed to know where everything was, moved about the house as if she'd grown-up next door and spent her best-friend time here. Did I ever sort out my surroundings as quickly, as easily? How did she get so sure so fast, so comfortable with herself? Opinions clear, freedom embraced, her place in the world unquestioned. How did that happen so early?*

Yet, none of her sureness, the snug fit of Kim in her skin, had been tested. No dead or divorced parent to retard its development, no apparent peer discrimination to challenge it, no real loss to test its strength.

No loss. It struck Sharon as oddly foreign. A *break-up with a girlfriend, sure that hurt, but who else did she know who had never experienced real loss? Not death, or divorce, or financial disaster. She could think of no one else. A grandparent Kim had never known, gone before she was born, didn't count. You can't lose something you never had. No true sense of loss. Foreign.*

Sharon adjusted her position, draped her arms over Kim, who was totally engrossed in a movie that Sharon couldn't care less about. It didn't matter. For now the feel of her, snugged in tightly, and the smell of her hair, sweet and familiar, was enough. The face that lately haunted her days and nights was gone, the ugliness of hate and death and injustice replaced, at least for a little while, with thoughts of pleasing and pleasure.

For a while, milk smooth skin yielding to her touch beneath crisp white cotton would be enough. She would see only Kim, only a lover, wanting her touch, needing her touch. Needing nothing else, only the simplicity of sex, primal and pure, nothing more. Untethered hands, untethered thoughts. Energy focused and driven, seeking one common end, finding one common end—simple, clear, uncomplicated.

Words had failed her more times than she could count, but her hands, they never had. They told what she couldn't say, showed what can only be felt. Sharon lowered her lips to the tender warm skin just below Kim's ear, and kissed her slowly as Kim snuggled in tighter, let her hands begin their message, let the movie end.

And when it had, Kim moved with intent. In an instant she was straddling Sharon's lap, breathing urgency hot against her face and pushing Sharon's hand through the open zipper into a quickening heat that still surprised Sharon. *So hot, so fast.*

Kim lifted, pushed Sharon's hand into position. "Ohh, yes," she said, sending the words toward the ceiling as she pressed down to bring Sharon inside. "Yes, baby," the words breathed hotly against Sharon's ear, "oh, yes." She lifted her hips again, just enough to keep the fingers from leaving, to keep them there against the sensitive place that Sharon knew well. Right where Kim wanted her, needed her. And she told her so, over and over, pressing down hard, taking the fingers deep again and again. "Yes, you know . . . oh, baby, yes . . . you know."

Sharon did know—had always seemed to know—exactly what her lovers needed, exactly what Kim needed. And their pleasure, Kim's pleasure, was intoxicating. The sound of it, in soft moans and excited breaths, warmed Sharon quicker than alcohol. She was lost in the feel of her, crisp white shirt open, smooth warm breast teasing, then demanding her mouth, her tongue. Lost in the rhythm, as it quickened and pushed its demands against her body. It was taking her there, taking them both to the edge—driving them hard, just as they wanted—so hard, so fast.

Sharon grasped the back of Kim's neck and pulled her mouth to her own. Guttural, urgent sounds escaped between kisses—kisses, frantic and deep, that took Sharon's tongue deeper each time. Hips matched each thrust of her tongue, as Sharon's hand slid easily in the wetness. So close, oh, so close. The rhythm ground down over Sharon's hand, driving it between her thighs, sending her own desire racing out of control. And for a moment, just a moment, there was a conscious, selfish thought to slow it down, let the intensity burn just a little longer. But seconds later it was gone, drowned in quickened gasps and the rhythm of hips racing to the edge. Sharon couldn't stop it, wouldn't stop it.

Kim grasped the top of Sharon's shoulders, pressed down hard and tilted her head to the ceiling. The sound alone, unbridled and throaty, was enough to send Sharon following her over the edge. Sharon pushed her hips up strong against the pressure and buried her own shout into the collar of Kim's shirt. She pushed up again and again, while the spasms shook them, took them helplessly to the end.

Kim collapsed against her, held Sharon's head to her chest. "Ohh, baby," she breathed softly. "Stay right there . . . it feels so good ... so good."

Yes, if only she could stay right here, in this place, drunk with her need—letting the urgency, the immediacy, ground her and hold her there in the pure goodness of it. If only she could stay right here, desire pounding against her, in her, forever. But, that wasn't possible.

They shared the rest of the night in pleasing and pleasure, while the rest of the world went on without them. The morning, Sharon knew, would bring her back to the struggle, front and center. Her escape over. So she needed to make the best of tonight.

Chapter Three

The atmosphere around the dining table strained for normalcy. School papers lay in front of Cayley untouched. Deanne sat at the end of the table and waited as Sage paced the length of the room and read the letter from Cayley's teacher.

Sage handed the letter back to Deanne and took a seat at the table. When Cayley met her eyes, Sage asked, "Is there something you want to tell us?"

Large brown eyes shifted momentarily to Deanne and back again. Cayley shrugged her shoulders and said nothing.

Deanne fought a smile. She wasn't as good at stifling it as Sage, but she knew that she had to for now. At almost seven, Cayley was already making the dynamic between mothers and daughter very interesting. *There was a lot of Sage Bristo in little Miss Cayley.*

"How many notices did your teacher send home with you before she had to send this to us in the mail?" Sage asked.

Cayley held up two fingers.

Sage nodded, leaned back in her chair and glanced quickly at Deanne. "So, this meeting your teacher wants to have with us is about something that you didn't want us to know about."

Cayley's nod was barely detectable.

No lies, Deanne mused, *the big rule hadn't been broken. A huge point in favor of lenience. So far, so good.*

"Did you think that if you didn't give us the notices, your teacher would just give up and we wouldn't know what this is all about?"

Finally, softly, "Yes."

"Next time," Sage said, leaning forward into a more intimate posture, "if there is a next time, just come to us and talk about it, because chances are that it isn't as bad as you think it is."

A more vigorous nod this time.

The ring of the cell phone, always clipped to Sage's waistband, halted the next, the inevitable, question. Sage checked to see who the caller was. "Sharon," she said to Deanne. "She'll keep calling until I answer."

"Go ahead, it's fine."

"Cayley, will you and Momma Dee talk about this so that I can take care of Sharon?"

"Okay."

As she passed by Deanne, Sage said, "She must be alone tonight. I'll be a while."

"Okay," Deanne said, standing and extending her hand to Cayley, "let's go sit on the couch and talk."

☙ ☙ ☙

"Hey, Sharon."

There was a hesitation that spoke louder than an actual greeting. *It was indeed going to be a while.*

Then, the slowly trailed together words that had become all too familiar. "I'm online . . . I don't . . . see anything yet."

"There probably hasn't been a decision made yet, Sharon."

"I check all the sites . . . you know, every night . . . yeah . . . I check every night."

"I'm sure you will know something before I do. Why don't you give me a call as soon as you know the decision." Sage heard the tell-tale sound of a pull-tab and envisioned Sharon sitting in the dark room with the light of the computer screen bouncing its blue-gray glare off her face. Whatever number of beer cans that it took for her to call had collected on the floor beside her chair, and it was just shy of eight-thirty. Cutting this call short, Sage knew from experience, would only result in another call. She settled back into the big leather office chair and turned on the computer.

"I want you to know," an unmistakable sip and swallow, "how much I respect you, Sage . . . I don't think I told you—"

"You have, Sharon. I know you do. You don't have to tell me. We just do what we have to do, don't we?" Sage pulled up an LGBT blog she liked to follow, and searched the recent posts for news of a decision from the governor. Nothing.

"Yeah," a long audible sip, "we do, we do . . . We'll keep on, Sage. That's what we do. For ten years, right? Even before that . . . It's been ten years, Sage. 1999."

Oh, yes, it was going to be more than a little while. And yes, it was a frustrating history.

". . . not one piece of hate crime legislation reached the President's desk . . ."

Sage turned the speaker on her cell phone off, held it to her ear and wandered down the hallway to check on the discussion in the other room. She quietly made her way past the deserted dining room to the family room, and peeked around the corner. The sight made her smile—Deanne and Cayley sitting close together on the couch, speaking softly, eyes resting easily on each other. A bond—sure and strong and safe—the family she never thought possible. The family she would never take for granted. *If only Sharon had the same peace.*

Halfway back to her office, her cell back on speaker, Sage heard the pull of beer tab number two. Total count, unknown.

"I really respect you, Sage . . . if I could do more like you . . . you know . . . if there's something more I could do . . . If I had the money . . ." another sip, another swallow, "I'd do like you . . . you know? I'd give some to each of 'em . . . each one fightin' for us."

"Well," Sage relented, "it takes more than money. It takes people like you doing the legwork, the grass-roots work in the trenches—canvassing, writing blogs and letters, talking—even when people don't want to hear it. It takes people like you just as much as it takes money. Don't forget that."

Clearly more at ease, Cayley snuggled against Deanne on the couch. "There," Deanne began, wrapping her arms around Cayley, "now, what does your teacher want to talk to us about?"

Cayley's arms tightened around Deanne's waist. "About not going to the library. I don't want to go to Media Time any more."

"Hmm, well as much as you enjoyed Mrs. Hanson's lessons on African animals, I'd say you must have a good reason not to go."

"I do," Cayley said, sitting straight up. "I liked lots of the lessons—the ones all about animals, and how the salmon swim upstream to lay their eggs, and I liked the one about the space shuttle."

"So, what happened?"

"I didn't like the lesson about Indians. It was wrong. The guy on the DVD called the women squaws, and he said their duties were like the colony women. And there were other things wrong, too."

That Cayley would have spoken up about the inaccuracies was not in doubt; how she spoke up was. "Did you wait until the end of the presentation and raise your hand?" Deanne watched her nod, and couldn't help envisioning an insolent Cayley biding her time through the rest of the lesson. The folded arms, the scowl, her disapproval would not have been hard to spot. "And, did you use a polite tone of voice?"

"Yes. But they laughed at me." The scowl appeared, no doubt just the way it had at school. "I told them in the Iroquois Nation the women of the council make the important decisions, and then they tell the chiefs what to do. When they laughed, Mrs. Hanson just smiled and let them."

"She didn't say anything?"

"Not to the class. She wanted to know where I heard that. So, I told her from my lessons on the reservation and my Nu' ye. She said 'you might have gotten things mixed up' and that's when I got mad."

"What did you say?"

"Nothing."

"You just decided not to go any more."

"Are you and Nu' ye going to make me go back?"

"I think we need to meet with your teacher and Mrs. Hanson before we talk about that."

ભ ભ ભ

". . . all those tries," another sip. "Damn, Sage, all those failures . . . I think . . . it's gonna go down again."

"Look, it's never gotten this close before. This is the best chance it's ever had. Don't pronounce it dead until it is, it's still alive on the Senate floor. It's going to happen, Sharon, if not this time, then the next. We just have to keep at it, and not let a defeat knock us down." Sage continued to check the blogs that she knew and trusted. No word of a decision on Crawford.

"No, it can't go down . . . no . . . what more can I do, Sage?"

Sage tipped her head back and took a deep patience-feeding breath. "You're doing it. Everything that you've been doing, just keep doing it. Let's concentrate on Crawford right now, okay?"

"I'm checking again . . ." a long pause, a long sip. "I don't see anything—"

"There hasn't been a decision yet, or it would be all over the blogs. I've checked, too, and there's nothing yet. Try to relax, okay? Go put on a movie that you know will put you to sleep. There's nothing more we can do tonight."

A loud sigh. "I can't sleep." Then the pop of another pull tab.

Number three, or is it four? Sage got up again and started down the hall.

"They don't know, Sage . . . People like Kim, they don't know."

The front room was empty, Cayley in the bath, Deanne laying out tomorrow's clothes. The regimen, the one they had structured with love, would be followed and respected. Safe and intimate, it was time set aside for winding down from the day, cuddling in and reading. And it had been sadly missing from Sage's own childhood. Just knowing that it was there for Cayley went a long way in making up for that.

Sage headed for the kitchen, still listening to Sharon and her somewhat less than sober remembrances. She was right, though: the organizations had been young, fledgling; the supporters nervous and unsure of what would happen to them. *It can't get scarier than taunts and threats escalating into violence—fists, and baseball bats and guns. And when someone gets shot for doing nothing more than speaking out in public, it gives validity to every threat from that point on. To stand and speak out again on those same streets had taken guts.*

"They don't know how scary it was then . . . you know . . . we were scared. But we stood up . . . that was scary shit . . ."

"Yes, it was," Sage replied, retrieving a bottle of water from the refrigerator. "It took a lot of brave people to get to where we are now."

Sharon's sigh dropped into a groan. "I don't know . . . brave? Do you think? . . . I don't know."

"Yes, I think so. You knew the risks, being out there and visible, speaking out, and you did it anyway. I'd say that's bravery."

"Yeah . . . but, it's not enough . . . you know. What else can we do?"

"I think we should get a good night's sleep for starters."

"Yeah, yeah, okay . . . I'll let you go. I'll check the sites again."

ೞ   ೞ   ೞ

"Sorry, honey," Sage said as she made herself comfortable on the couch and laid her head on Deanne's lap. "How did single-parenting go?"

Deanne placed her book on the lamp table and ran her fingers through the short brown waves of hair just above Sage's ear. "One, or both, of us need to meet with Mrs. Phillips tomorrow, if possible."

"Do you think we both need to go?"

"No, but you might want to be the one to meet with her. Cayley and I had a good heart-to-heart, and I think she needs to know that you understand what she's feeling."

"Which is?"

"An awakening to second-class citizenship."

"Already? What the hell happened?"

"Well, our daughter decided that she would no longer attend the Media Time in the library and was caught sort of hiding out in the bathroom."

"Really," Sage replied with a frown. "I didn't skip my first class until I was in the eighth grade—hanging out with Paula Singer. Stealing forbidden kisses was temptation enough for me to chance Mrs. Barker not believing that I was sick in the bathroom. There was true hell, though, to be paid at home if I was caught."

"It was tenth grade for me—Mrs. Selby's P.E. tap class. I got seasick watching her flabby thighs. There was something very wrong about a P.E. teacher with flabby thighs. So, since I couldn't concentrate on her feet long enough to learn the steps, my best friend and I decided to spend the hour eating cheesy fries at our favorite diner downtown."

"So, what was so . . ." another frown, "whatever, that Cayley felt the need to skip Media?"

"Three times."

"Before she got caught?" Sage's smile was slightly disturbing.

"Yes, and wipe that smile off your face. You have some work to do."

"You throwing single-parenting back in my lap?"

Deanne pulled a pinch full of hairs over Sage's ear. "No. You're better equipped to deal with what pushed Cayley's little buttons. Evidently, the librarian was reading some stories about Native Americans and they saw a DVD about the colonists and the Indians, and what Cayley took away from the experience was that they thought Indians weren't very smart and that the women were subservient. When she tried to correct the inaccuracies, she

16

was laughed at. She got upset and decided not to go anymore."

"Wow," Sage replied softly. "That snuck up on me."

"She's heard everything you said. She knows exactly who she is. The problem, as I see it, is that no one else does."

Sage nodded. "I'm thinking we're going to want more than one conference at school . . . and, I'm thinking again about how important it is that we have the rest of the family here. It's the kind of support, of validation, that no one else can give you. It's what I didn't have and what I want more than anything for Cayley."

"*I'm* thinking it would be as good for you to have them here as it would be for Cayley."

Sage tilted her head so that she could look directly into Deanne's eyes. "I do long for more time for Cimmie and me to enjoy just being sisters, and to get to know Jeff as more than only a brother-in-law . . . Maybe watching Lena be a grandmother to Cayley would even help me see her as my mother. *And* I know without a doubt, there is no better support for Cayley than having Naline to go to school with—a year apart, a common heritage, neither of them alone in knowing who they are."

"Give them a chance, honey. Both Cimmie and Jeff are seriously looking at options."

"I'm not sure Jeff really understands how important it is. I feel like I can only say so much. I have to leave it to Cimmie."

"Then do that, and try to relax. For right now, everyone is fine. The girls are happy and doing well in school. Things will work out." She smoothed her fingers over Sage's forehead and her cheek. "I'm not worried about Cayley at all," she said and kissed Sage's forehead. "Sharon, however, can give cause for worry. Tell me what's going on."

Sage sat up and shook her head. "Drinking, obsessing, lonely . . . I can't not take her calls."

"I know."

"I think she feels I'm the only one who'll let her talk politics for so long."

"She's right."

"Probably, since Laura's been gone. But, as much of a pain in the ass as Sharon can be, she does make me want to find a way to do more. To go back to the days when marching and being physically visible made me feel vital and effective. You can't throw money at a governor's decision. It takes time, commitment, visibility."

"We could all do more. But, we have to find what we can afford to give without shortchanging our families or our jobs."

Sage shook her head. "I don't think Sharon *could* give any more. It's consuming her. For a while there it seemed as though she had it balanced. Her depression seemed to be under control— *you* know, she was showing up for card nights, making rude jokes. But, this early release thing is really kicking her butt."

"She'll get through it, honey. She has good friends around her."

"I don't want to watch her self-destruct again."

"That's why you'll always be on the other end of those eye-rolling phone calls, because she needs you to be."

"I never thought I'd say this, but I wish she'd walk into next card night, laugh that ridiculously infectious laugh, and pull some awful practical joke on someone. I wouldn't even mind if it was me."

Chapter Four

The voice from the cell phone pierced the fuzz of Sharon's hangover. "Well, thanks for finally answering your phone. Dammit, where are you?"

"Comin', Kase." *As fast as this old buggy can get rollin'.* "I'm on my way out the door." She downed the glass of Alka-Seltzer in one breath and shuddered. *Miracle fizz. You've got one hour to make me human again.*

"—still there?"

"Yeah, Kase." She grabbed a bottle of Gatorade from the refrigerator and locked the back door.

"Four calls, Sharon. It took four calls to get you to answer. What the hell's going on?"

Sharon fumbled with her keys and they dropped to the gravel beside the truck. "I overslept again." *That would be finally slept. Sometime after the shiver and the spill, came the collapse of the deacon's one-hoss shay.* Sharon bent down to retrieve her keys. The bowling ball inside her head hit the back of her face. She bit hard into her bottom lip to prevent a long, loud complaint. "Everything's fine. I'll be there in fifteen minutes."

"No. Just go right to Lowe's. We've lost enough time this morning. You're almost out of mud. Pick up what you need to finish so you don't have to make another trip. And get enough baseboard for the front room. I couldn't salvage any of it."

Sharon climbed painfully into the truck. Everything hurt. *Someone did a shitty job of putting the shay back together.* "Anything else?"

"Of course. But we can't put anything more on the account until the end of the month, and I need you *here*."

"I'll be there as soon as I can." *Not like before, Kase. Not like before. A little depression—well, more likely just a full case of anxiety. And, who wouldn't be anxious? Waitin' to see if some murdering son of a bitch is gonna go home? Have his family hovering around him, tellin' him how much they love him, how they wish they had more time with him. No fucking way that should happen. So, who wouldn't need a couple of beers to get to sleep? How much good am I gonna be with no sleep, eh, Kase?*

Ș ʘ Ș

Kasey met her at the back of the truck as Sharon slid the second of two fifty-pound buckets of drywall compound to the edge of the tailgate. While Sharon coaxed painful knees down from the truck, Kasey wrestled the first bucket onto the handcart.

"They sure as hell come *down* a whole lot easier than they go up," Sharon grumbled. "There's something in my DNA makeup that just can't let me stand around past ten minutes for some knuckle-dragger to stop countin' stock to load two lousy buckets of mud." She grabbed the second bucket and dropped it with a thud on top of the first.

Kasey turned the handcart and started toward the house. "Yeah, it depends on what time of the day you're there."

"It depends," Sharon replied, following her with the bundle of baseboards, "on if you look like you or you look like me—but it didn't take today to turn that lightbulb on. I guess I'm just in no mood to put up with it today."

"Your knees hurting?"

"Screamin'. They're going to be cursing me every time I crawl up that damn pick today." *To say nothing of my head.*

"Maybe if you had been there earlier, there would have been someone available to help load."

Yeah, right. "Loading two damn buckets of mud didn't do the damage. Puttin' this old body back on active duty did. Any chance we can hire a little grunt help?"

"We're in deep shit, Sharon."

"How much deeper can it get? We dropped five employees in sixteen months."

"If we had the money for grunt help, it should go to Troy. We're paying him half what he made before he got laid off, and no health insurance." They pulled the cart up the plywood ramp and rolled it into the hallway. "We've got to get these two houses done and rented by the beginning of next month. And if we can't sell the other two, you and I aren't going to be pulling a salary for quite some time. That's how deep it can get."

"I know, Kase."

"Then you also know that drinking every night until you can't get to work on time's not going to get the job done." Kasey turned to leave, but stopped. "When does twice a week become a pattern?" She shot a hard look at Sharon and left the hallway.

Right to the point. Expected. Unnecessary. "I'm here, aren't I?" Sharon yelled after her. "Bad knees, bad head, bad whatever. I'm here," she yelled one last time before grabbing a bucket, muscling it into the room and onto a tarp. "It's my company, too." Sharon snipped the edge darts, hooked her fingers under the lid and began forcing it open. "Like I'm gonna let it go down." She pried stubbornly. "She knows better than that. Shit!" Her fingers slipped painfully from under the lip. "I'm in no mood for this, either."

With a rush of ire-laced adrenaline, she grasped the edge of the lid with both hands and ripped it back. The pain from her fingertips was easier to tolerate than the pounding in her head. "This room'll get done today if it kills me." She picked up the drill motor with a groan, worked the paddle into the compound, and began mixing. "And kill me it might."

Hours later, Kasey emerged from the basement. "You ready to break for lunch?"

"Go ahead. I'm not hungry." Sharon made a long smooth pass with the wide knife and moved further down the pick.

"Well, take a break and have something to drink with me."

Still no eye contact, and another long smooth pass along the seam. "I'm fine. Go ahead."

Kasey left the room and shouted back, "I won't be gone long."

It wouldn't matter whether she was or not. The plumbing would get done in its right time, Sharon knew. If it took Kasey five more hours or ten, if it took until one in the morning, or all day Sunday, the precious only day off she had promised to Connie. Kasey would get it done, Sharon was never in doubt of that.

What bothered her most was that after all these years of working together, Kasey didn't have the same confidence in her. No—more honestly, what bothered her most was that she had given Kasey reason for that lack of confidence. It was the spiral again, a force of gravity, pulling her into depression, striking her shins and knocking her to her knees. But, this time it came out of nowhere. She'd learned to handle the losses—speak her mind, vent her anger—she was able to control it again with jokes and laughter, normal days, normal nights. She'd gotten past it before. Mom's death. Ronnie's death. Close family all gone—and Donna and Evonne. All the sadness and the anger and the soul-paralyzing grief—she'd gotten through it all. *So what is this in comparison? Just some evil old man about to take his last breaths somewhere undeserving. Leave it to the organizations like Kasey does, like Kim does. Let them do the work, trust them to make it right. Why isn't that enough?*

"Hey." Kasey tapped Sharon's calf. "Come down and talk to me?"

She looked down at Kasey's uplifted face and nodded.

While she made her way across the pick and down the ladder, Kasey placed scrap squares of drywall on top of two mud buckets and sat down.

"The next thing you're gonna have to build me is a damn access ramp to that pick."

"Then we can patent it and sell it to geriatric drywallers."

Sharon finally smiled. Still *we,* always *we.* She sat opposite Kasey and accepted the cup of McDonald's latte. "I'm sorry, Kase," she said, holding the cup in both hands and staring at the lid. "I don't know what's wrong with me. I can't get things out of my head." Eyes up, only a second, then refocusing on the coffee lid. "You know, the tough things, at night when I'm alone. This early release thing has brought it all back."

"I know, Sharon. You don't have to talk about that."

"But I do. Things don't bother you the same way they do me."

"They bother me if I let them. I make myself concentrate on something else—or I talk about something else, or I sing. That probably helps me more than anything."

"So, you don't want to talk about it because you don't want *me* to think about it, or because *you* don't want to?" Blue eyes, thoughtful eyes met her own. Truthful eyes. She counted on them, believed them.

"Both—I guess. I know how to take my own pain away, but I feel so helpless to relieve yours. I don't know what to do, how to help you. And I want to—you know I'd take it away if I could."

"But it does help—talking to you. At least I think it does."

"What helped—finally—was seeing Dr. Talbot, and getting medicated."

Sharon stood. "No. I'll take care of it myself." She turned her back, placed the coffee on the pick, and started toward the ladder. "I'm not taking the drugs again."

"Why not? They worked."

"They made me feel like a damn zombie—like there were parts of my mind that I couldn't find anymore, and not just the painful parts. I don't know how to explain it."

"And your choice of self-medication is better? How'd your head feel this morning?"

"At least I know what to expect—and I can sleep at night. You don't know what it's like, you've got Connie there every night."

"It'll get better, Sharon. Give it time. You're finally dating

23

someone instead of satisfying the occasional urge. That's going to help, even if she is only fourteen."

Expected. A jab to the obvious. Lift the mood. "She's twenty-eight."

"Same difference. But give it a chance to help."

"She's not there every night. I'm not ready for her to be there every night. And if I've learned one thing in these past few years, it's that my need to talk about something doesn't mean that it's good date conversation. It took a few date-killers before it penetrated the oak pulp between my ears, but I think I finally got it."

"But that's part of who you are. How's Fourteen going to get to know who you are without knowing what's important to you, or what you've been through?"

"Yeah, so how do I know when I start sounding . . . obsessed or something?"

"Self-absorbed, you mean?"

"Yeah, self-absorbed. Like all I'm interested in is how *I* feel and what I think is most important."

"I guess it's been so long since I was actually dating that I don't think about stuff like that anymore. How *did* I talk to Connie about things that bothered me?" She raised her eyebrows and slowly shook her head. "I guess I didn't. Connie *pulled* it out of me, inch by inch. Now that I think about it, it was a pretty painful process. Like finding splinters and pulling them out."

"Well, mine just stay in there and fester. That's why talking to you is important to me."

Kasey nodded, dropped her head momentarily, then looked directly at Sharon. "But, I don't know what more to do when you're numbing yourself with alcohol."

Numbing, yes, that's exactly what she was doing. Talking wasn't enough, wasn't easing the angst or arresting the anger. As much as she wanted it to, depended on it to—it wasn't enough. Numbing it worked. There's no denying it. It wasn't pretty, but it worked—at least at night.

"I'm not a professional, Sharon. And I don't want you to rely only on our friendship and then not get what you need. I can tell you what I think or what I see, but I'm afraid you don't take it seriously, like you would from a professional."

"I listen to what you say, and I do take it seriously."

"Then remember what state you were in six years ago, and promise me that you'll do whatever it takes to keep from going there again."

The damn cavern, with mile-thick walls—unpenetratable—no one in, no one out. Deadened space that suffocates hope and aborts dreams before their first breath. Nothing in, nothing out. The cavern that swallows you whole. How could she forget? She wasn't going there.

Chapter Five

Something woke her, maybe a skewed internal clock, but something made Sharon sit straight up in bed so fast that the room felt like an out of control merry-go-round. Even blurry, bloodshot eyes couldn't miss the bad news glaring at her in large red numbers from the alarm clock.

"Shit!" she shouted, stumbling out of bed and steadying herself against the nightstand. "Ah, dammit!" Her head pounded fiercely as she grabbed the same clothes that she had just crawled out of a few hours before, and pulled them back on. "She's gonna be pissed. *So* pissed."

She scooped up her cell phone from the nightstand and for a second was tempted to call Kasey. *Right. What am I gonna say, the obvious? I'm two hours late to work, but I'm sorry? Yeah, sorry, good choice of words.*

"Shit, just get your sorry ass in the truck," she muttered. Without a thought to grab the bag of tools with her eye protection and respirator from the garage, she climbed behind the wheel and backed out of the drive. "I promised her it wouldn't happen again. *Promised* her." She slowed the truck only enough to check for traffic, then rolled through the stop sign. "She's counting on me. What the hell's wrong with me?"

The traffic infractions continued until she reached the busier areas of town and the unavoidable traffic lights. "Just couldn't remember to set the damn alarm. Everything would have been fine, but no, just couldn't do it . . . *Dammit!*"

Halfway down the block a sign caught her eye. Krispy Kreme,

Kasey's favorite. The decision was a quick one. Sharon pulled in, parked, and hurried into the gas station. *Perfect.* She grabbed a plastic bag and two each of Kasey's favorite donuts.

"It'll be fine," she promised, climbing back into the truck. "I'll work through lunch. Hell, I'll work all night. It'll be fine."

☙ ☙ ☙

She had nearly convinced herself that it not only would be fine, but that, like two days ago, it would be merely a matter of an awkward half an hour or so before everything returned to normal. *If I can just deal with this super-sensitive, throbbing mass that took the place of my head.*

But the moment Sharon walked into the house, she realized how wrong she was. The rented floor sander sat in the hallway. The old carpet and padding had been cut into three-foot wide strips, rolled and taped, and Kasey was bent over pulling staples from the hardwood floor. All of which Sharon should have had done while Kasey was cutting and replacing the damaged sections of floor with new oak boards.

"Damn, Kasey, I'm sorry." Sharon placed the donut bag on the floor next to Kasey. "I'll finish that up."

Kasey continued pulling staples and made no indication that she knew Sharon was standing there.

"I forgot to set the damn alarm. Why didn't you call and get my ass out of bed?"

"I'm not your mother."

Right. You're my very pissed-off business partner. I knew that. "I'm sorry. I know you don't want to hear any excuses. I guess I really don't have any, anyway. Look, I'll work through lunch. I'll stay as late as it takes. I won't put us behind."

Kasey kept working.

"Hey, I brought you your favorite Krispy Kremes. Take a break, while I load these rolls into the trailer, and I'll finish the staples. Okay?"

Kasey finally stood. She left the pliers on the floor, and picked up the bag of donuts. The only eye contact she offered was when she handed the unopened bag back to Sharon. "This is just another fifteen minutes I could've used your help."

CR CS CR

This morning had been the proverbial straw, the last, lonely, left to fend off fate as long as possible, straw. And now it was gone. Sharon needed no further proof of that than the clear lack of normalcy. No conversation, or chitchat; no laughing, no spontaneous song out of Kasey.

Sharon worked through lunch, sucked down a whole pot of coffee because she hadn't grabbed her bottle of Gatorade, and allowed Kasey her distance. Her physical discomfort took a back seat to her emotional misery.

She guided the sanding machine over the old floor. The dust seeped around the edges of a cheap dust mask while the whine of the motor pierced her unprotected ears. The pain in her head screamed for relief. Her own fault, all of it—the hangover, the respirator and ear protection left in her garage. Punishment of her own making. The worst punishment, though, was the disappointment she had seen in Kasey's eyes.

Sharon finished vacuuming the last stretch of the sanded floor and shut off the shop vac. She couldn't take it any more. She ducked through the plastic sheet covering the doorway and went out the side door. *This is what she wants, this is what she'll get.* She dug her cell phone out of her jeans pocket, searched her contacts, and made the call.

Minutes later, she ventured into the basement. The fumes from the PVC cement were overpowering. "Whoa, Kase, time for a break. This shit'll give you a permanent pass to la la land."

"I'm fine," she replied, circling the end of a pipe with cement and twisting it into an elbow.

"If you say so . . . Hey, I got the floor done and the room

28

cleaned. I'm gonna get the baseboards cut now, but I wanted you to know that I called Dr. Talbot. I'll take the next opening she has, unless that will put us too far behind."

Kasey stepped down from the ladder, a look of surprise on her face. "No, it'll be fine."

Sharon nodded.

"I should have the plumbing done tomorrow. We can make up the time, it's not a problem."

"Yeah, I'll get myself straightened around, Kase. Then we'll kick the rest of this out. You'll see."

"That's what I'm counting on." She screwed the top down tight on the cement and grabbed a rag for her hands. "Come on. I need fresh air, I'm losing brain cells."

Chapter Six

"Okay, so look," Sharon began, sitting lightly on the edge of the chair facing Dr.Talbot. "I promised Kasey that I would come and talk to you. And lately, with my promise-keeping battin' average, I couldn't start in the Pee Wee League. So, I'm really glad you had a cancellation and could get me in."

Dr.Talbot's neatly cut bob was more salt than pepper now, but when she smiled the creases around her eyes were as warm and welcoming as when Sharon first met her. Really, it was that smile that had brought Sharon back after her first visit—easing upward into compassion, creasing its promise to help into soft lines. She believed what it told her. "Any time you need to see me, Sharon, just call. I don't mind flexing the schedule."

"It's not like before." Sharon said, easing back into the chair. "I need to get back on track, that's all—reassure Kasey that everything's okay. We're both carrying a pretty big workload. She has to know I'm not gonna let her down."

Dr.Talbot lifted her chin, her eyes remained fixed on Sharon's. It was the look that said, *You might believe what you just said, but I don't.*

Sharon broke eye contact, dropped her gaze to her hands smoothing themselves over her knees. *It's not like before . . . it isn't.*

"*Situational* depression," Dr.Talbot began, sitting across the corner of her desk from her client, "can come on suddenly. It's not unusual for it to be triggered by a related event or even the fear of one. The fear of an early release could certainly cause it.

Not being able to focus on anything else, and the lack of sleep that you talked about, may not seem as bad as it was before, but it will escalate if you don't address it right away. Have you been able to sort out your thoughts like we worked on during your earlier depression?"

Sharon shook her head. "No. Nothing makes any real sense— I shouldn't be depressed, I should be angry. Why aren't I just mad as hell that he might get out?"

"You are angry." Dr. Talbot hesitated, made sure that she had solid eye contact. "What would you do if you were *only* mad as hell?"

"I'd be there when they brought him home." Her voice held the tone of contempt barely in check, her eyes fixed into a hard stare. "And I'd blow a hole in his chest big enough to shove my fist through."

Sharon shifted her eyes to the orange and black movement in the large fish tank against the wall, and set her shoulders at a defiant angle. Enough time for her to own her words. *What does it mean when you say that shit out loud?*

"How do you see him?" Dr. Talbot asked. "Like he was the last time you saw him—still capable of killing someone else?"

"I see him as an evil, self-righteous son of a bitch. That's how I see him. The only difference between Charlie Crawford and Charlie Manson is that Crawford didn't have the opportunity to kill as many people."

"Are you afraid that he's still capable of killing someone else?"

"I know where you're pushin' my thought process. He's old and sick now, there's not much chance of him being 'pushed over the edge' again. But capable? Hell, yes, he's capable. You can't convince me that if he had a gun in his hand and someone who looked like me standing within range that he wouldn't absolutely shoot. He sure as hell would shoot."

"So, if you *were* there when they brought him home, and you blew that hole through him like you want, what makes you any different than he is?"

31

"Nothing," Sharon replied quickly. "Not a damn thing, except that my self-righteousness would do the world a big favor . . . But, I guess the real difference is that someone taught me that you can't go killin' people just because you don't like 'em. So, you don't have to worry about your professional obligation, or whatever it is when you have to decide if you're gonna call the police to report that your client is talking about killing someone."

Dr. Talbot smiled. "No, I don't worry about that with you, Sharon. You have a very strong sense of right and wrong."

"So, is that my problem?"

"Do *you* think that's your problem?"

"Well, something sure is. I got anger I can't do anything about, injustice I can't do anything about, and loss that I can't do anything about—except pour alcohol over it."

"You are doing something about it. You're here. We'll work this out, Sharon. Some things take time and can't be done alone, and that's okay."

"Not when you're running out of patience."

Dr. Talbot relaxed more comfortably into her chair. "We all lose patience at times. But the mind is a complicated thing. There are no simple black and white, right or wrong solutions."

"I always thought I was rather simple to figure out. Everyone seems to know what I like and what I don't. Even kids and dogs got me figured out."

"Dogs?"

"Yeah, you know, people say that when they die they want to come back as a lesbian's dog. I can't keep the neighborhood dogs from camping out in my yard. I got one that sleeps on my back porch, and a pup that races across the street every time I come home. I don't even feed 'em, they just want the attention. They just know I love 'em."

The doctor smiled. "There's a lot to be said for pure, unhampered instinct. We'd probably all be better off if we could get closer to our basics."

Basics. How much closer to basics can a threadbare jeans and

T-shirt lesbian get? Zero to low maintenance. Suave shampoo, hamburgers, and Bud beer. Simple. Basic. Sharon tapped her finger against her temple. "This is not a complicated mind."

"Your *uncomplicated* mind has a permanent record of everything that's ever happened to you. It's all stored there, an indelible account of everything you've ever seen and smelled and heard and felt. An overwhelming amount of data, so overwhelming that if you recalled it all you'd be doing little of anything else. So, you recall what's necessary when you need it. At least most of the time."

"That makes sense. I don't need much."

"I said most of the time. There are times when you try to recall something and can't. It's there, you just can't consciously pull it up. And your brain can also repress memories that are too painful for you. A balance that gives you time to gain skills so that you can handle and understand what happened."

"So what happens if your mind doesn't do that for you?"

"Repress the uncomfortable memories for you?"

Sharon nodded.

"Sometimes you find a way to suppress them, pushing them out of your conscious thoughts, replacing them with less painful thoughts."

"Kasey does that, my friend Kasey." Sharon pushed back hard in her chair. "I can't."

"Are these thoughts about bad or sad things that *could* happen, or *have* happened?"

"I see their faces, every night when I can't sleep. Donna and Evonne, laughing and teasing, like the last time I saw them, telling stories to embarrass each other. And I see Ronnie with that smirk daring me to one-up the last prank he pulled." For a moment she stopped, her lips forming just a hint of a grin. Then it was gone. "I'm glad they wouldn't let me see him after the accident. I wish I hadn't seen the bike. I wish the last time I saw my mother alive she wasn't lying in a hospital bed struggling for each breath. I was useless; I couldn't do anything to make things better for her."

"And Donna and Evonne?"

"Useless, totally useless. Just a tit on a bull. I couldn't do anything to help any of them . . . Or maybe I could have, and didn't. I heard what they told me, the things that he said to them. They even warned me to stay clear. But, I was all about me, me not being afraid of him, not letting him scare me. *Me.* I was so busy denying him *my* fear that I didn't see how dangerous he was to them. Stupid. I was stupid and useless."

"What do you think you could have done, Sharon?"

"I don't know exactly. Make them file more police reports? Maybe they shouldn't have engaged him at all, just ignored him completely, no matter what he said or did. I don't know, is that even possible day after day? That's why I thought a six-foot fence was the answer. But, maybe that only made things worse. Maybe he didn't want a resolution."

"Maybe. Even in retrospect, there is no clear resolution that would have changed the course of events. There's no way of any of you knowing what was going on in his mind. You couldn't know what had happened in his life to shape his thought process or trigger a violent response. At the end of all that retrospection and second-guessing comes the realization that there are things that happen in life that you personally cannot prevent. And with that realization comes a kind of peace."

"That old saying about knowing what we can change . . ."

"Exactly. And the fact that it is best known as a prayer tells us how difficult it is to do that by ourselves."

"That part might not be so hard. I get it that I'm not Superwoman. But, I can't even fix the things that I should be able to change."

"Then that's what we'll work on."

 α ℭ α

"Hey, where are you?" Sharon called, as she made her way down the hallway.

"In the kitchen," Kasey replied.

She was bent over some paperwork spread out on the counter when Sharon walked in.

"Ah, so this is what really goes on when I'm not here."

"Trying to figure out how much we can pay on our account so that we can get enough insulation for the attic." Kasey straightened and tucked the pencil over her ear. "What are you doing back here anyway? You didn't blow off the appointment, did you?"

"I went, I went. Damn, I just thought we could still get some work done today."

Kasey put her hands up. "Let's take a breath and start again. Thank you for going. How did everything go?"

"I did go for you. You know that, right? I can't keep disappointing you, letting you down." Sharon held up her hand. "You don't need to say anything about promises I've made. I know I need help. I wasn't going to admit it. I was just gonna go once, get my mind straightened around again and make you feel better."

"Did you make another appointment for next week?"

"And the next week and the one after that . . . I can't keep going like I've been."

Kasey finally smiled. "I made you a partner in this business because I need you—more now than ever."

Sharon nodded. *Smart woman. I need her to need me. I need to be a part of why this business is going to make it through. My needs and she knows them. But I don't even know what she gets from a partner worth half her salt and a friendship too needy to enjoy. When's the effort going to be way more trouble than it's worth?* "I know." She titled her head back and puffed out her cheeks. "But, I don't want to take these damn drugs, Kase."

"What's your alternative?"

Her voice was low, her tone unpretentious. "I don't know. I just don't want to feel like this anymore."

"I know you don't." Kasey's voice went right to that place, right where it was expected, right where it was needed. It stilled the turbulence and set the ground beneath Sharon's feet.

Chapter Seven

How long had it been, six months? No, more than that since Kim Blake had become a regular part of Sharon's life. No earthquake tremors had accompanied her, or 4th of July fireworks. She had merely appeared at the Outloud Chorus benefit, sat down and started talking. As simple and easy as that. And, just as easily, Sharon had welcomed the quandary of her, young and sure, very different and strangely appealing. She didn't understand it but, for whatever reason, Sharon had let her in. Maybe she'd figure out her own reasoning some day. Right now, though, she didn't care why—it didn't seem to matter. They do what they do, have what they have, and for now that's enough.

The last hard-strum note of the electric guitar hung momentarily over the small gathering of women crowded around the little tables in the s'aut room across the courtyard from the 'aut bar—the hub of the gay and lesbian community. Following its ebb was an enthusiastic applause and an elbow to Sharon's arm. The performer with the backward baseball cap was smiling her thanks and Sharon was facing Kim's annoyed scowl.

"Not clapping is rude," she said, leaning past Sharon's ear. "At least pretend until we get outside."

"Oh," Sharon replied, quickly clapping. "Sorry."

"I might as well have been here alone tonight for all the fun you've been. Is there something else you'd rather be doing?"

"No, no." Sharon stood as the others began to move about. "Let's get a sandwich in the bar."

Spring air cooled quickly this late in the day and ushered them to the bar through the communal space of the courtyard. Paved in old brick and dotted with trees and patio tables, the remnant of an ancient street now connected the flow of activity between reclaimed two-story houses. The tall narrow houses were now homes to various community organizations, the bar, the bookstore, and an activity center. It was the core that embodied community awareness and connection and involvement. A visible, tactile alternative to the ever-increasing realm of the internet. Time spent here was palpable therapy for the hours Sharon spent in front of the computer screen.

They ordered and settled at a table near the window overlooking the courtyard.

"I should have asked Kat and them to come," Kim was saying, "I wouldn't be talking to myself all night."

"It was okay tonight, like I said. I like it better when they don't try to sound like someone famous. But I already told you that."

"No, you didn't. You're talking in your head. Where's the 'nothing can touch Motown' oration I've come to expect? Musical genius. The rhythm of a thousand dances. Arrangements requiring people to really know how to sing. Come on."

"You've heard it all before."

"But I'm ready with new comparisons—Mary J. Blige, Beyoncé. How can I argue with you when you're talking in your head? If that's what those meds are doing to you, you need to flush 'em and smoke a little weed."

"They take the edge off. I've been really upset about that bastard, and you don't want to hear about it . . . Nobody does."

"You've got to let it go, Sharon. Live *your* life. Be happy. Why do you even listen to the news? It's just a bunch of negative crap that you can't do anything about anyway. All it does is crank up the angst to Prozac level."

"Zoloft."

"Whatever. The point is that you do it to yourself. You've gotta let go of what you can't change."

"I'm getting pretty tired of hearing that from everyone. We

can do more than I ever thought we could. Hell, we have a black president. I never would have given that a nickel's chance in Vegas."

"I know—I vote. And if I'm lucky, enough others voted the same way and we put people in place to do what I can't do myself. I want to do more with my life than worry about all the injustices in the world. All my growing-up years I had to listen to my dad rant at the TV—as if spoiling his family's evenings was going to change what the news reporter was saying. It was senseless, and I won't ruin my enjoyment of life like that."

"So, we're right back where we started. I shouldn't have talked about it in the first place."

"Look, I want to kick your ass at paintball, laugh at your totally inappropriate jokes, force you to eat ethnic foods, and keep you up all night having really good sex. I do not want to talk about politics, religion, or anything that I can't personally do anything about. And I don't want to be talking to myself for *another* three weeks while you're taking a magic carpet ride."

"Damn, you know, I wish you'd be a bit more specific. I hate to always have to guess what's going on in that head of yours."

Kim remained in her usual semi-sprawl position, arms draped over the frame of her chair and feet resting on an empty seat, as the waiter delivered their food. "Specifics," she said, "keep you from wasting time going down dead-end streets."

"Yeah, well, specifics have gotten me into trouble so many times that I can't *specifically* tell you."

A smile, infectious and revealingly young, widened the band of fawn-colored freckles over Kim's cheeks.

Sharon swallowed a bite of burrito. "Oh and, magic carpet ride? That's more than a little before your time."

"I teethed to Jefferson Airplane, Black Sabbath, Led Zeppelin, Jimi Hendrix," she replied between bites. "My mom's an old hippie. Well, actually my dad, too, but he spent more time getting tear-gassed and arrested while my mom was getting in touch with her inner spirit . . . yep, she's back in fashion. At least, her earth and social consciousness is. Her fashion sense is still a little iffy."

"So, I take it that your mom knows that you enjoy the wacky weed on occasion."

"Where do you think I get it? I told you it's as pure as it comes. She grows the best."

Sharon shook her head. "I can't imagine my mother . . . I think the only law she ever broke was doing 35 in a 25."

"She doesn't sell it, Sharon, she grows it so that my dad will chill enough to enjoy the good things in his life. He relaxes, plays his guitar for my mom, puts in time in the community garden. I wish they'd smoked more when I was younger. He's a really cool guy when he's not stressin'. I'm telling you, you should give it a chance."

"And I'm telling you that you're wasting your breath. I'm no longer a smoker, and I'll *never* be a toker."

Chapter Eight

Sharon pushed the coins into the meter as fast as she could. Her attention was focused on a small crowd of protesters gathering across the street from the County Building. A local news van sat in front of the building's entrance.

Left on the truck's seat was her notebook, a short piece of 1 x 6, and her original intent, a list of materials to pick up at Lowe's for the rest of the day's work. A phone call halfway there had changed that intent.

She raced to the edge of the parking lot toward the inter-section and the voices of the women grew louder. Disjointed shouts, out-of-synch attempts at chants. "Do the crime—do the time." "No excuse for hate." "No early release." Something slammed hard against the inside of Sharon's chest. Despite the pills, their effect kicking in weeks ago, mind and body reacted immediately, adrenaline finding its level and fueling her mission. She stepped from the curb, anxiously waited for traffic to clear.

The group was small, she knew each of them. They'd grown older, grayer, heavier, but like herself they were no less committed, no less passionate. They saw her now, running toward them against the light, and they met her at the curb.

"What's this about?" Sharon asked, quickly hugging one of her oldest friends. "Why isn't he getting interviewed in Lansing? And how the hell did you find out this was happening?"

"Jan was in the clerk's office when she overheard the women behind the counter talking about Crawford's son and the news crew. She called me, and then we just started texting everyone we could. Why *here,* I don't know."

Another woman added, "He's trying to get some public sympathy because Crawford is supposed to be dying."

"So the media shows him talking 'family' right here in the backyard of the murders," said another. "Sort of redirecting the focus."

"They *want* it to be about Crawford," Sharon said. "Somebody come up with some paper and a marker, here," she directed.

Her intent was clear. Various pieces of paper, typed one side, office notes, and a marker appeared as the news crew sprang into motion. Sharon turned Jan around and used her back as a clipboard. She wrote quickly, handing out each of the papers with a name on it.

"Everyone thinks it's about Crawford, but it's not," Sharon added as Jeremy Crawford emerged from the County Building. "It's about Donna & Evonne. It always has been."

"And Matthew, and Richard," said another.

"And Suzanne, and Christine, and all the others that we can't let them forget."

"Exactly," Sharon replied, "exactly." She pulled her wallet from her pocket as the news reporter began his interview. She walked toward the intersection where she was intercepted by one of the policemen assigned to keep everything civil. She raised her open wallet and shouted across the street, "Remember these faces. Remember these names."

The women stepped to the boundary held by the officers and the name signs surrounded Sharon. The chant began. "Remember these faces," as Sharon thrust the picture in her wallet upward. "Remember these names," and the name signs shot upward.

Over and over, louder and louder, as the interview went on and Jeremy Crawford calmly made his plea.

"Remember these faces. Remember these names."

Twice the cameraman panned the little crowd of protestors,

recording names, recording faces. Twice they were more than heard. "Remember these faces. Remember these names."

Then only minutes later, the crew was packing up their equipment and Jeremy Crawford was gone. There was nothing left to do but to go home. But then, Sharon knew, it would be time to re-group, re-organize, and once again plan an old-fashioned, grass root kind of visual protest and figure out where to take it next. She needed to get bodies out from behind the safety and convenience of the computer, to put to use every bit of today's technology to mobilize real bodies, real faces, not the innocuous images on Facebook pages and fleshless names on petitions. *When did we start hiding ourselves away? When younger leaner, bodies seemed to be defining what they were instead of who they were? Did we miss their purpose, feel left behind? Or did life just selfishly claim so much of our days that we found ourselves settling for the internet and what was left of our nights?* Whatever it was, she knew of nothing written in stone that said that it had to remain that way. What she felt right now wouldn't allow it.

Exhilaration. Hell, yes, that's what it is. Sharon bound across the street and into the parking lot. *That's exactly what it is—energy-filled, rarely felt exhilaration.* Her thoughts began jumping on top of one another, each vying for prominence, the next challenging for priority. There were people she needed to see, phone calls and e-mails to be made. Donna's daughter, Evonne's brother. The group was so small now, relying for so long on technology to make their messages known. She needed to see their faces, hear their voices.

She was nearly to her truck when she saw him—same sportcoat, same thinning hair, on the far side of the parking lot. It wasn't a conscious decision to keep walking, to arrive at his side, to confront Crawford's son face to face. She just did it.

"Do I know you?" he asked.

Sharon produced the picture once again. "Not any more than you know these two women."

"Of course I know who they are," he replied with a disarming tilt of his head.

"But you don't *know* them," Sharon insisted. "You don't know what they meant to me, or to their children or to their families. You couldn't know any of that and ask for their murderer to be given any kind of mercy."

He made no attempt to open his car door, just slid his hands in his pants pockets. A momentary silence offered little relief for either of them. Then he lifted his right hand from his pocket and offered it to Sharon.

"I'm Jeremy Crawford," he said. "And you are?"

"Determined to make sure that that murderer never gets an ounce of mercy," she replied without shaking his hand.

He returned his hand to his pocket. "You're right," he said, "I didn't know your friends. I don't know what their loss has meant to you. I can only imagine—"

"You can't imagine, you haven't even tried."

"And you don't know my father, or me, or *my* family."

"I know all I need to know. Your father walked up to my friends and shot them to death in cold blood. He has no right to live. I just want you to know that I will do everything I can to help make sure that he dies alone in prison."

Sharon turned abruptly, giving him no opportunity to continue the conversation, and marched to her truck. Accomplished—strike it from her jumbled, still unprioritized list. She took the opportunity when it presented itself. The exhilaration continued.

ଔ ଔ ଔ

"Jesus, Kasey, you're not going to believe . . ." the words tumbled forth, explaining the delay, the fervor, the new mission.

Kasey listened, perched atop a short ladder, plumbing repair suspended. "Was Jenny there?" she finally managed to squeeze in.

"She and Brad took the kids and their friends camping. I'll fill her in on everything when she gets back. 'Oh and by the way, when you were camping your mother's killer's son was on TV, asking for a pass for his father.' "

"Have you heard from Donna's brother in a while?"

"He's in North Carolina. He stays involved in the effort to get the Hate Crimes Bill passed, but when I e-mailed him about Crawford he just said 'thanks for letting him know. Nothing else."

"Have you ever thought that over the years he's been able to forgive him?"

"No way, Kase. It's not forgivable. How can you even say that?"

"Because he's never seemed the type to let anger eat away at him."

"Like me?"

"I didn't say that."

"You didn't have to."

Chapter Nine

"Laura! Laura! Come here, hurry."

The urgency of her mother's voice brought Laura Jamison bolting into the front room. "What is it? What's wrong?"

But Adele Jamison wasn't lying on the floor, or in distress as Laura feared. She was sitting on the edge of her chair and pointing at the television.

"Hurry, it's Sharon. Sharon's on the news."

And there she was, an instant later, up front leading the chant—that look in her eyes that cleared away all the debris, the one that could buy forgiveness for even the rudest of practical jokes. The look of intent, colored bold with passion. It defined her. It told the world of the crusade at hand. It told Laura much more.

"It's about those women you knew who were killed." Adele was pulled up close to the TV, watching intently.

Laura watched from behind the chair, unable to turn away, and wishing that it were only because of them that she couldn't.

"Do you really think they would let him out early?"

Laura's response was quick with unexpected pride. "Not if Sharon has anything to say about it."

"She's a good leader, don't you think? Getting everybody's attention like that."

Standing up, calling out the injustice, taking it on with no reservation—yes, she's good—strong, articulate, fearless. Laura had been forwarded the e-mails, seen her name on all the online petitions and blogs to pass the Hate Crimes Bill. *How many letters must she have written, how many trips to marches? Tireless for* the cause. *There was never a thought that that would have changed about her. If only Sharon could bring it home, narrow it down, and take it on face to face, one to one. If only . . .*

"Laura, honey?"

"I'm sorry, Mom. What were you saying?"

"Nothing. I was just thinking that you should call Sharon."

"Mom—"

"Just think about it, okay? It's been a long time. I still get a card from her every birthday and every Christmas. She never misses."

"I'm not surprised."

"Anyone who is that good to your mother should at least be a good friend, don't you think?"

"You are assuming that she would want a friendship."

"Of course I am." There was that all-familiar intonation, the Mother Superior of her childhood, despite the confidence nearly waned from her by barely controlled complications of diabetes. It made Laura smile.

ରେ ଓଃ ରେ

"Connie," Kasey called from the kitchen, "turn on the news."

"Already got it," she replied. "You don't think I'd miss the combustible Sharon Davis, do you?"

Kasey draped the dishtowel over the drying dishes and hurried into the living room. "I don't know which will earn me a halo faster, dealing with Sharon the Depressed or Sharon the Crusader. One has me worrying about bailing her out at work, the other worrying about bailing her out of jail."

"Shh," Connie replied, grabbing the back of Kasey's tank top and pulling her down next to her on the couch. "Look for Sharon."

It had been dealt with years ago, all those emotions, the tears, the empty space where two lives had been. Echoes of laughter fading with time, visions of loving smiles thinning. Dealt with,

46

but not gone. It took only a moment, only the cameras focusing once more on a face too close to a memory and the protesting shouts of passionate women.

Kasey stared at the screen as if the years hadn't happened at all. As if trying to keep a business afloat and a relationship strong hadn't managed to self-level the void created by one man's hatred. This man's father.

"I understand how upsetting this might be to some," he said. "What my father did was inexcusable, but that was not the father we knew growing up. He was not right, emotionally or mentally, when he took their lives, and he has paid for that with as many years as he could. He's dying now."

"There are many," the reporter replied, "that will say that ten years in prison is hardly enough payment for two lives."

"It's not for him that we're asking for his release. Our family has suffered loss, too. We've lost those years with our father, and he has great-grandchildren who don't even know him."

"But the victim's families will never have that chance."

Jeremy Crawford lowered his eyes and nodded. When he lifted them again to the cameras he said, "If I could in any way change that, I would. But I can't. We're only asking for mercy, to let a sick old man go home to be with his family when he dies."

The camera made another pass over the crowd of women, still chanting, still demanding to be heard. But Kasey turned her head, first toward Connie, then away.

"There's our girl," Connie said, as the camera zoomed in on Sharon and the picture in her hand. "She sure knows how to nail a foot to the task, doesn't she?"

But Kasey made no response, her forearms resting forward on her thighs, her gaze fixed in an absent stare.

"Kase?" Connie reached out, gently stroking the back of Kasey's head. "Are you all right?"

Kasey responded by turning to lean into Connie's embrace. She tucked her head into the curve of Connie's neck and wrapped her arms around her.

Connie held her like that, stroking her fingers through the short blond hair, and whispered, "I'm sorry, honey."

ଔ ଔ ଔ

The soft red glow of the clock marked time in minutes, normally unnoticed even in the blackened bedroom. The minutes moved one o'clock to two while Kasey fought the grip of a paralyzing silence. No laughter to mask the sadness, or work talk to crowd out the memories. Nothing to keep Evonne, with her husky laugh and irresistible glint of mischief, to keep her from telling her again about the 4th of July party she was planning—the plans she would never get to finish. Or to keep Donna, blushed and excited, from showing her the ring she bought for Evonne's birthday, just the right one—the one never given, never worn. The memories came, one leading to another, and then another. Off-key sing-alongs and horseback riding. Confidences and unspoken trust. The little things like a compliment at just the right time, and big things like accepting Connie without hesitation. Everything that made them special, that had seated these women solidly, permanently, as an indelible part of Kasey's heart.

But it was a part of her life where a phone call for a little reassuring advice or the sound of a needed laugh couldn't happen anymore. And the instinct to pick up the phone was gone, too, finally. Who they were, though, will always be.

Chapter Ten

Sharon pulled the truck into her drive, cut the engine and opened her door to a wiggling, whining ball of multicolored fur standing on her hind legs and making it nearly impossible for Sharon to step down.

"What am I going to do with you, little girl?" She carefully got out, and to a chorus of barking from across the street, she bent to receive her greeting. "You dug yourself another exit, didn't you?" She said as the wet tongue flicked over her lips and chin. "Yeah, I know, I missed you, too. Okay, okay, let's get your ball."

The little dog easily beat her to the back porch, and began pushing her nose at the lid of an old wooden box.

"Someday, you're gonna get that thing opened just enough for it to snap back down on your nose."

Before Sharon could dig out the miniature tennis ball and get back down the porch steps the dog had already raced to the back of the yard and was poised at the edge of an overgrown perennial bed for the throw she knew was coming.

She caught the ball, thrown just hard enough to make the distance, returned to drop it at Sharon's feet, and raced at flat-out speed back to her post for another. Her excited anticipation made Sharon smile, and watching her return throw after throw, over and over, gave Sharon a joy surpassed only by the days of her youth. Each breath felt young and new and brought back the smells of summers long ago when promises swung on the tails of kites and laughter rippled water like skipping stones. *If only living could be that simple again.*

What would I be willing to trade for that paper route and shiny black Schwinn? For secret forts and games of Ditch'em, and no more sleepless nights? And, if it were possible, would I?

She never knew how many throws it took, only that when it was time for another break the little dog always let her know by bringing the ball back and dropping on top of it. Sharon filled a bowl from the porch with fresh water from the hose and sat on the bottom step to watch her drink.

"Yeah, I think I'd trade it all . . . well, maybe not you." Sharon gently stroked the soft hair on the pup's head until she finished drinking. "No, I'd steal you away from ole Hank and once you were mine I could give you a proper name. Yeah, I'd trade the rest of it and you and I would jump in the truck and go wherever we wanted . . . Until then, though, come on, little girl," she said, picking her up onto her lap, "I've got to get these burrs off of you . . . Oh yeah, these damn stick-me-tights will mat this pretty hair up so bad we'd have to shave you bald. And you're such a skinny little thing under all these curlies, it just wouldn't be a pretty sight."

She began working diligently, between wet kisses on her face and a tongue in her ear, to carefully separate each tiny burr from the fine hairs. "You're probably wondering how my day was today, weren't you?" Halted kisses and a serious tilt of the little head. "Well, I would have had more fun tunneling under old man Jenkins' fence. No media excitement like I told you about last time. Nope; while you were diggin' a hole halfway to Shar-Pei land, I was bustin' my butt to fill the trailer for a dump run before the realtor got there. Our last-ditch effort to sell that place before we rent it out."

She finally worked the last of the burrs from the hair on the little dog's legs and rolled her onto her back to tackle the ones on her belly. "Have I told you how much I hate being a landlord? Oh yeah, late rent, no rent, partial rent. That mortgage payment's still got to be paid on time. And they break things and leave the place filthy. Then I go back in there and fix everything all over again. Frustrating. Like having to dig a damn tunnel all over again because I filled in your last one," she said and smiled. "But, I do that because I love you. What would I do without *you*? You are the absolute best listener—even better than Laura, and that's goin' a stretch. Someday I'll tell you all about Laura—all the things nobody else wants to hear . . . There you go. What a good girl. You deserve a really good belly rub . . . and you're reason enough to weed Laura's garden and get rid of those damn stick-me-tights."

Laura's garden. It'll always be Laura's garden—planned and planted, weeded and watered—by Laura. And struggling now through sporadic and haphazard care to show its splendor. The sunny yellows, pale lavenders, and pinks of the spring crocus and tulips splashing their colors freely before the weeds try to choke the summer brilliance of lily reds and rose pinks. And every fall the mums and asters struggle harder for their survival. "Yep, I'll weed it Sunday, just for you."

ভ ভ ভ

It wasn't hard to find the new escape route, it wasn't far from the last tunnel under the chain-link fence that Sharon filled with big rocks just days ago. They were only temporary stopgaps she knew, but it wasn't her fence. And until she could convince old man Jenkins into a better solution, this was the best she could do.

Accompanied by a pack of five jumping, whining dogs all vying for her attention, Sharon stepped carefully through a fecal minefield and made her way to the back of the old man's yard. She picked out two more good sized rocks and forced them deep into the hole, stomping the dirt in around them.

"There," she said, giving each head a fair scratching, "that'll keep you busy while I try to talk the old man into something else."

"She git out again?" He was standing on the back stoop, an old sleeveless undershirt stretched taut over his belly. "Don't make no sense that the rest of 'em don't follow her."

"I guess they know she's my favorite. But, I worry about her getting hit, Hank. Why don't you just let me buy her from you?"

"Nah, she helps keep the varmints outta the yard."

"I don't think she does much of her share, she's at my house so much."

"Well, I'm kinda partial to her, too. But, you come over here and play with 'em all you want."

The same thing he told her last week and the week before that. "Then I'm gonna have to bury some chicken wire below that fence if you wanna keep her from getting out."

"Ain't got money for that right now."

"I got some left over from a job. I can get the front here. I'll pick up some more next week to do the rest. You don't have to pay me for it. I just don't want her to get hurt."

Chapter Eleven

How much longer can I avoid it? Another week? With a little luck, maybe another month? Laura stood in line at the prescription counter, unwillingly tempting fate. She was in the wrong drugstore in the wrong part of town to think that luck would hold much longer.

One more person in front of her and then she could pick up her order and be out of there. She wasn't in any way prepared to run into Sharon, or any of them. Not yet.

She glanced carefully over her shoulder, checking the visible aisle of low shelves behind her with the cautious stretch of a turtle ready to snap back into her shell at the first sign of recognition.

And snap she did, a second later when a familiar profile rounded the end of the aisle. Her first thought was to disappear behind the next row of shelves and head for the exit, but the pharmacist's voice stopped her.

"Prescription for Adele Jamison," he said, far too loudly.

Laura stepped to the counter quickly, fumbling to retrieve bills from her wallet.

"How is Mrs. Jamison doing?" he asked.

"Oh, somewhat better. Just the co-pay?"

"That's it," he replied. "Great program for seniors. I was so glad to see this go into effect here."

"Yes, yes," she said, collecting the envelope from the counter.

"Will you tell Mrs. Jamison that George is asking after her?"

"Yes, of course. Thank you," she replied with a slip of a smile and a quick turn.

But there, blocking her exit with no way to avoid her, was Kasey Hollander.

Laura offered a smile that was not returned and she felt the painful edge of apprehension slicing past her heart. A nod and a pass, she knew, was too much to expect. In her most accommodating tone, she asked, "How are you, Kasey?"

There was a hesitation, a second when the familiar blue eyes slipped a hint of their usual compassion. But they steeled again immediately. "I hope to God you are only visiting."

Her first temptation was to give an explanation, to justify—her second was not to answer at all. Laura settled for, "Will it matter what I say, Kasey? Is there anything I could say that would change what I'm sure you think of me?"

"No. Nothing."

Laura lowered her eyes and tried to step around, but Kasey moved to stay in front of her.

"What you *can* do is listen," Kasey continued, meeting Laura's eyes directly. "And you're going to. I never did get my chance at you—Sharon wouldn't allow it. No one could tread on Laura Jamison, not even Sharon. Not one negative word, not even after what you did to her." Kasey moved closer, her stare demanding attention, intimidating. "Not one in all this time. She protected you, protected some distorted, unrealistic image of you that she refuses to let go of. And it almost killed her."

The words made Laura's breath stop short of exhale. Her eyes bored into Kasey's, her brow knit hard above her nose. *It almost killed her? Was that really possible? Hurt her, yes—there was hurt all around. No matter what had happened between them, there would have been hurt. Kasey has it wrong, very wrong.*

"No. It was the murders, the depression. She needed help, Kasey, professional help."

"She needed her friends and her partner to stand by her, to see her through it. Not turn their backs and desert her. She deserved your loyalty, the same damn loyalty that she still gives you—but you gave her *nothing*. You turned your back and walked."

"If you're going to judge me, you should know why I left."

"See that's the problem, Laura. *You* think you have a reason good enough—*I* don't think there's any reason that can justify it. So don't waste your breath—just stay the hell away from Sharon. She's shaky right now, and if you push her over that edge again there will be no one capable of keeping me out of your face."

"I have no intention of trying to see Sharon and I don't need you to tell me that that's the right thing to do."

"Really? Well, you're here, and if she knew you were . . . This time I guarantee you, you are not going to destroy what it took years to put back together."

Laura's response, had she had the time or words, would have been to Kasey's back. She had, evidently, given her message, wanted no reply and was on her way out of the store.

Kasey's reaction wasn't a surprise; she was as good a friend as Sharon could ever have. Always watching out for her, protecting her. A bond there as thick as blood. Their friendship challenged any lover to care as much, to stay as long. There were no surprises there, either. It had been clear from the start, from that first inkling of interest, that Kasey Hollander was an important and permanent fixture in Sharon's life. And nothing was likely to change that.

For months now, since she knew she had to be here for her mother, she knew this day was coming. It was inevitable that she face Kasey, that she hear what she assumed put into words. And, now that she had heard them, faced Kasey eye to eye, it was over. The others, eventually even Sharon, would be told that the message had been delivered, and they would have their discussions and they'd analyze Kasey's rendition of a reaction, and maybe eventually they'd all stop talking about it.

The worst of it was that it still mattered—what they thought. What they believed. It made her quiver with the need to explain—to somehow make it just and reasonable in their minds. But she couldn't; she was frustrated into silence, still trying to untangle reason from emotion in her own mind. A task she had, until now, abandoned, and one that she still doubted could ever bring peace—to anyone.

Chapter Twelve

Sharon accepted the bag of Aleve and Mountain Dew from Kasey as she slid behind the wheel of the truck. Words from Kasey, "Subway okay for lunch?", but no eye contact.

"Yeah." She saw her, too. The tone of her voice was unmistakable, and the profile—sternly rigid, unblinking—said all that was needed. "I saw her go in the store, Kase."

Still no contact. Kasey turned her head, backed out of the space, and started toward the parking lot exit.

"It's all right, Kase. I'm okay." *The quivering in my gut will go away. My heart will stop pounding. I will be okay. I will.*

"I confronted her." Kasey's focus remained on traffic. "But I wouldn't have told you if you hadn't seen her."

Sharon nodded. "What did you say to her?"

"Just to stay out of your life."

"It's coming back to haunt me, isn't it?"

Finally eyes straight on met Sharon's. "What is?"

"The way I treated Connie in the beginning."

"You were wrong, but you did it for the same reason I did . . . why, do you think I'm wrong, too?"

"Does it matter?"

"Not if you believe her when she says she has no intention of trying to see you."

"She said that?"

"Yes."

Of course she did. Don't be stupid—even for a second. She's probably been in town before, to see her mother, visit friends that she used to work with. We just happened to see her this time. Not a problem. She has a right.

"She looked good, though, didn't she? Lost weight, cut her hair." Immediately, Sharon wished that she hadn't said it out loud.

"So does a deluxe hot-fudge sundae to a diabetic."

ↂ ↂ ↂ

The feeling had bothered Kasey all afternoon. She'd seen the look on Sharon's face, recognized it, and chose to shade it with a thinly disguised sense of self-righteousness. She couldn't stand to see it—the glint of hope in her eyes—futile. *Totally futile. Someone had to keep the light shining brightly, expose the flaws, protect her, even if it's from herself. And who else would do it?*

"I know that look," Connie said, circling the grill and removing the tongs from Kasey's hand. "That one that stares right at dinner as it cooks to a crisp." She turned the chicken breasts and pulled them to the edge of the coals.

"Damn. I'm sorry."

Connie slipped a hand around Kasey's waist and turned her. "What's bothering you?"

She offered a pitiful effort at a smile. "I feel like a shithead."

Connie gave her full attention as she always did, and the words came tumbling out as they always did. Seeing Laura, the ensuing come-apart, and "I took the floor boards right out from under Sharon's feet. No easing her down into the pit with a safety rope; no, I aimed between the eyes and told her that Laura had no intention of seeing her." Not at all the way Connie would have handled it. Emotion would not have been allowed to spill over the boundaries of acceptable restraint. She would not have been a "shithead, like I said."

"I might agree with you if I didn't know how much you care about her. But, I'm also not convinced that a more tactful approach wouldn't be just as effective."

58

"I've had these moments when I thought so, too. I look into her eyes and I know what's in her heart, and all I want to do is make everything all right for her. Then, I come to my senses and remember how easily things can turn sour and I know I can't sugarcoat it. For Sharon the point has to be filed sharp so that it penetrates deep enough."

Connie brushed barbeque sauce over the chicken breasts and nodded. "Maybe you're right."

"I am, but it doesn't make me feel any better."

They fixed their plates in silence and settled at the table on the corner of the sunroom. Next to the sliding glass door, the feline part of the family was already dining on precooked chicken. Meals were more peaceful when the girls—Juno, young and pregnant when they found her, and her daughter, Billie, named for her soulful voice—ate first.

Silences like this usually brought up each one of Kasey's work projects begging to be solved, and an analysis of finances trying to find their balance. Kasey's thoughts rarely left work freely, relying on Connie's coaxing to shift priorities. Today, though, they were fixed obsessively on Sharon and Laura.

Could the years away from Laura actually be a bad thing? Enough time for the negatives to be minimized or forgotten, allowing all their best moments to rise to the top like sweet cream. No reminders, nothing to reinforce the hurt and callous the sensitive places that leather gloves and steel-toed boots can't protect. What would happen if I kept my advice to myself?

Connie finally broke the silence. "So, what I'm deducing from all of this is that you don't think Sharon's relationship with Kim is strong enough to get Sharon through a Laura sighting?"

"We don't know that it will be one sighting. We don't know what she's doing here, or for how long."

"Things you probably could have found out if you'd had a civil conversation with her."

"That might have been my only chance to let her know how I feel. So I took it."

"That doesn't surprise me. You and Sharon are more alike than either of you will admit. And you still haven't answered my question."

"I can't answer it, that's why I'm worried." Kasey pushed the remainder of her pasta salad into a neat pile on her plate. "How many times have we done anything socially with Sharon and Kim?"

Connie shrugged.

"Two, three times," Kasey offered, "in what, six months?"

"Meaning?"

"Meaning that if it were more than a diversion she would be bringing her fully into her life. We are a huge part of Sharon's life, we're her family, and if there's one thing I know about Sharon Davis it's that she'll never commit to a relationship that doesn't include her family."

Connie nodded. "Any more than you could. And you know from experience how tricky that can make things. Prejudgments and assumptions can do irreparable damage."

"Yes, and I am very lucky that you loved me enough not to let Sharon scare you off."

"No irreparable damage because we both loved you enough. I hope there is someone like that for Sharon."

ଔ ଔ ଔ

"Shit, was that an aster?" Sharon knelt on one knee, relieving the stress to her lower back, but not the pain. She examined the leaves of the plant she clutched and wished she had paid attention when Laura had tried to show her the difference between the perennials and common weeds. The spacing, nearly obscured with overgrowth, convinced her to put the torn roots back in the ground.

The back garden hadn't been as difficult as this one. The stick-me-tights and catnip were easily distinguishable from the hostas and ferns. And the spring bulb section had been even easier. But, she was tired now, exhausted really, and couldn't remember what was what. And yet, something compelled her to get it done, all of it—not only the places where Hank's little dog chased the ball, but every bit of it—as if doing so would somehow please Laura.

Wasn't that what she'd been doing all day, all evening? Looking at the yard through Laura's eyes? Making it acceptable. Working until sweat stung her eyes red and her lower back stiffened near rigor so that Laura would approve. She was right here—present, almost palpable—knowing the effort, appreciating it, a whispered balm that soothed sore muscles.

She could hear her saying, "It's even pretty *now,* in the heat of the summer, after the spring bulbs are done. Look how the sun illuminates the yellow leaves of that hosta. And my favorite, the deep red of the Asiatic lilies. So beautiful," she would say, her tone hushed in reverence.

But, somewhere between the Asiatic reds and the junipers at the front of the house, the voice she heard changed.

"She has no intention of seeing you." *No intention. Kasey said it, no doubt why, only if—if Laura had really said it. If Kasey would dare to lie, even for what she thinks is the best of reasons. Hell, 'dare'? How dare I think that Kasey would lie to me? What the hell is wrong with me?*

Sharon threw the last handful of grass and weeds back under an out-of-control juniper and painfully straightened her back. "What the hell am I doing? Breaking my back for what?" For who, more accurately. Rightfully, for the personal pride of a well-kept yard, an esthetic and artistic statement, and for the maintenance that would keep little dogs free of burrs. Reasons that are acceptable, healthy. But that wasn't the case, and she knew it. And so the words burned in her belly: "she has no intention."

Of course she doesn't.

Sharon left the compost can where it sat next to the front steps and went inside. *Only a moron would expect differently.* She retrieved a beer from the refrigerator, then stood looking through the kitchen window at the backyard until the last bit of light left the day.

No intention. It was no revelation, but the words still kicked hard at her gut. Still they turned perspective ass-end up, and promised to torment her until she stopped them.

Chapter Thirteen

Too loud. Too loud. Stop shouting. The words kept bombarding her "Get up," they demanded. "Get up, Sharon."

But even if she willed it, the body still clad in paint-splattered cut-offs and sunk into the couch like a useless battleship, couldn't move. The disconnection was nearly complete. No feeling, no pain, no response. Only hearing remained. Stop, her fragmented mind pleaded. But the thought never found its voice, and the demands kept coming.

It didn't matter. They would stop on their own—the voice would soften to a pitying sigh and leave. It always did. It would leave her to her secret mission—the annihilation of memory, the cleansing—and then, like so many other things in her life, it would never come back. The final swirl of the downward spiral, dizzying and swift.

Kasey frantically searched the medicine cabinet in the bathroom, then hurried to the bedroom, searching the bedside stand and the dresser. "Where are they, Sharon?" she shouted as she rushed down the hall to the kitchen. "Where are the pills?" She shouted as she checked the counter, the garbage can, everywhere someone might leave a prescription bottle. Nothing. "You can't drink when you're taking those damn pills . . . dammit."

"The truck," Kasey muttered to herself. She raced out the back door to the driveway. "Please tell me they're in the truck." She flung open the passenger door and hit the glove compartment release. The white pharmacy bag was there, the bottle of pills only partially gone. "When the hell did you stop taking them?"

She made a hasty assessment that gave some relief. "Normally, I'd be pissed, but today . . ."

ଔ ଔ ଔ

"Okay, I know you're not dying on me, so get up, Sharon." Kasey's voice was firm, determined, bordering on angry. "Get up, dammit!"

Go away.

"You're not going to do this again, to yourself or to me. Coming to work hungover—not coming to work."

The words confused her. She'd heard them before. The same words, the ones from the top of the spiral. The same words, wrong voice. *How many times? How many different voices? 'Shut up,'* her mind shouted. *'Shut up and leave.'*

The pillow covering Sharon's head was ripped from under the heavy weight of her arm. Kasey's voice had settled into resolution level. "How's this helping? How's this making your life better? Huh?" She tossed the pillow toward a nearby chair, and cleared beer cans to the side with her foot. "This place reeks." Kasey bent closer to the motionless body on the couch. "And you smell like you died three days ago. Even in your most delusional fantasy you cannot imagine that Laura would want to come back to you like this."

Sharon opened her eyes at the sound of Laura's name, but quickly squeezed them closed against painful shards of light. She pushed blindly at the air in front of Kasey, and groaned. "Leave me alone."

"No. I did that last time, gave you time, let you have the space I thought you needed to get past it. Look what good that did. And here you go again." Kasey grabbed Sharon's legs and pulled them clear of the couch. "You're no good to anyone like this." She grasped Sharon's arm with both hands and hauled her into a sitting position. No effective resistance from Sharon, only another groan. "I know what loss is all about. You know I do. You've got

64

to get angry, somewhere along the way, you've got to get angry. And you can't do that as long as you're drunk."

ତ୍ର   ଔ   ତ୍ର

Promises hung unfulfilled in every room of Sharon's house. A bare sub-floor pleaded for new tile in the bathroom, lightbulbs dangled from pigtails in the kitchen, living-room walls waited for a final coat of mud and primer. Dust and disarray and dirty dishes glared at Sharon's shuffling indifference as she made her way from the bathroom to the kitchen table.

"How long you gonna camp out uninvited in my Hilton here?" she mumbled. "Connie know where you are?"

"Well, with that sunny disposition," Kasey leaned over Sharon as she dropped onto the chair, and sniffed freshly shampooed hair, "and the sweet smell of a clean body, how can I leave?"

"One out of two is all you're getting."

"I see that. . . . Here," Kasey plopped a plate on the table, "eat this."

Sharon shuddered and turned her head at the sight of the sandwich.

"Yeah," Kasey sat down across the table from her, "a shock to the system."

"What are you smiling at?"

"You're so easy. No mystery. No guessing."

Sharon frowned. "What does that mean?"

"I always know where you are, what you're thinking, what you're feeling. It's right out there plain and simple."

"Yeah, that's me," she said, picking up half the sandwich, "plain and simple."

"It's a compliment, Sharon. That kind of honesty is rare."

Sharon forced down one bite. "It's not honesty—it's stupidity. It's a damn bulldozer with one gear and no brakes. It's like my wiring's all backward or something—the control switch isn't activated until after I run over something."

65

"That's because honesty is sometimes hard to look at, it makes people uncomfortable. They'd rather you faked it or told little white lies. But, that doesn't make honesty less of a virtue."

"No. It makes it a deal-breaker. I can't fake it and I can't hide my feelings and it costs me. I guess I'm just too old and too stupid to learn." She picked up the sandwich, stared at it for a second, and returned it to the plate.

"Are you talking about Laura? You can't be suggesting that she left you because . . ." Kasey stared from beneath a fiercely knotted brow. "That was depression, Sharon. You know that. Situational depression. Having your best friends murdered will do that to you." She stood, the burst of emotion coloring her cheeks. "Leaving you sure made that better, didn't it?"

"Don't, Kasey." She dropped her head and buried her forehead in her hands.

"Somebody has to. You'll stand there with the house falling in on you, trying to keep the debris from hitting some plaster idol of Laura. Damn, Sharon, why can't you see that?"

"I gave her more than enough reason to leave."

Kasey's voice rose with emphasis. "And to stay." She turned abruptly, cleared the sandwich makings from the counter and shoved them into a nearly empty refrigerator. Sharon never moved.

"The person you still love," she said in a quieter tone, "is not the Laura that you fell in love with."

There's only one Laura. The Laura with eyes that really saw me; that looked beneath the sixty extra pounds and barely forgivable social graces and saw something that she thought was worth loving. It isn't her fault that she kept her eyes open. Or that what she saw wasn't so loveable.

"Maybe it's just me," Kasey was saying, "but I believe when you agree to a committed relationship that means more than just being monogamous and committed until life gets a little rough or uncomfortable. Isn't that what you thought you had?"

Thought, assumed, took for granted. Sharon remained silent, motionless. The droning in her head muffled what few thoughts she did have. And anger promised too much pain. There was no challenge to her self-loathing.

"She bailed on you, Sharon. Things got a little rough and she bailed. Left you to deal with the grief and depression on your own—because it was easier." She threw her hands up and turned away from the table. "Selfish," she said sharply. "Totally selfish. That's not what love is."

Sharon shot from her chair. "Stop it! Just stop it!" Her cheeks quivered, her eyes painfully defied the fluorescent glare. "I can't help how I feel. You can't change how I feel. So leave it alone— leave me alone!"

"I will not. You don't mean that and you never will. We'll get through this together like we've gotten through everything else. We both know that undying loyalty of yours is both the best and the worst of you. So, if it takes getting mad at me for you to move on, then so be it. You're not going to be left alone."

Chapter Fourteen

"Laura, can we skip our walk today? I'll do a session on the exercise bike tonight instead."

Sliding two chilled water bottles into her pack, Laura ignored the temptation to slip from physical therapist to daughter mode and give in to her mother's request. "Until I get a treadmill in here for you," she replied as she emerged from the kitchenette, "there's no substitute for walking. It's not only cardio we're after, it's weight-bearing exercise. Remember what I—"

"I remember." Adele Jamison pushed herself up from her favorite chair with a groan. "I've got diabetes, not Alzheimer's. I wanted to have my friend, Mary, over today." She accepted the wooden cane from her daughter at the doorway. "It might do you some good to have more of a social life."

Laura took her mother's elbow and ushered her down the step to the sidewalk. "I had dinner with Dave and Sue from work just Tuesday."

"You know what I mean. You're too young for this." She labored under the weight of years of excess pounds to make her way down the sidewalk. "Too young to be alone."

"You let me worry about my love life."

"*Are* you worrying about it?"

"I'm worrying about you right now—getting you as healthy as possible and avoiding another comatose stint in the hospital. You, my dear mother, are too young for this."

Too young. What a ridiculously relative term. Is it really any more acceptable to bow under to the failures of your body at sixty-one than it is at seventy-one? Less traumatic, or less of a loss to those who love and depend on you? And if you're partly to blame because you let your weight get out of control and dismissed telling symptoms, does it stop the ripple of consequences from touching others?

Her mother's grip tightened on Laura's arm, pressing down harder now with each step. Testimonial breaths prayed hard for ease and, like her own three years ago, gave their inadequate best. Her mother stopped, blew a thin vapor of air through her lips and looked at Laura.

"Do you think I can lose as much weight as you have?"

"That depends on how badly you want to."

"What made you stay with it long enough this time?"

Laura nudged her mother forward. "I was fooling myself for so long. I didn't get honest with myself until a patient let me know that I wasn't fooling anyone else. He asked me if I needed to take a break during a therapy session when I was manipulating his lower back muscles. I must have been huffing. It was really embarrassing."

"Well," Adele paced her words as she paced her steps, "if embarrassment . . . was what it took . . . I'd have lost weight long ago."

"Embarrassment only made me honest. I didn't get serious until my own diabetes diagnosis."

"You don't want to be like me."

Nearly blind, kidneys compromised, heart weakened. No indeed. "No more than you don't sometimes." They made their turn to start back at the gate to the complex pool. "But, we're doing something about that. Right?"

Adele nodded without looking up.

"And, there are a lot of ways that I wish I were more like you."

"Oh, sure, my Hollywood looks and operatic voice."

"Yes, there's that." Laura smiled, stretched her arm around her mother's shoulders and squeezed. "And your sense of commitment and your sacrifice."

Adele stopped and looked at her daughter. Those words contradicted a belief that had been set years ago. Little in the time since had done anything to alter it. It surely wasn't respect that had driven her children from their house at the earliest possible opportunity. And it seemed that only a sense of duty had brought them back together on holidays. There was love, even if rarely spoken of out loud, but acknowledgement of commitment or sacrifice? Not one.

"Come on," Laura said, "let's get in and settled and get something to drink. We didn't walk long enough to drink what I brought along."

ભ ભ ભ

The conversation that Laura had needed for a very long time had finally begun. She pulled up the large worn footstool and sat in front of her mother's chair.

"I need to ask you something," she began. "I've wanted to for years, but it never seemed to be the right time." Concern was evident on her mother's face. "Why did you stay with Dad all those years?"

Concern changed quickly to something that most resembled relief. There was no hesitation to her answer. "Because I loved him."

No, much too simple. Not an answer that could even begin to cover all the childhood disappointments, or the teenaged embarrassments. A little girl will forgive more than once because she loves her daddy—a hug, a new promise, and a treasured gift, no matter how late, turn tears into a smile. Belief still trumps doubt. Childish hope that soon dissolves into adolescent embarrassment. Love struggling to overcome an intoxicated father at teacher conferences, refusing to endure bringing friends home. A hard love to hold.

"But you must have wondered what your life might have been like with someone else. Didn't you get tired of making excuses, of shouldering the financial burden for the family?"

"Nothing's easy, honey. Every family has its challenges. There are burdens out there that I'm grateful I didn't have to bear."

"But, didn't you ever wonder?"

This time a little hesitation. "There was a time . . . you kids were all real little. I thought hard about our lives. I thought for weeks. I'd sit on one of your beds each night and watch you sleep, and go over what I knew in my mind. I looked for what I knew was true. I knew he loved me. I knew you kids were the most precious things in his life. And I knew he was an alcoholic. I knew that none of these things were going to change . . . I had to decide."

"If you would leave him?"

"If love was enough to stay."

Laura slowly shook her head. "See, that's what I never understood. I guess I still don't. It's not a tangible thing like staying because it's financially easier on the family. That would be easier to understand. In my teen years it was all about me, you know, how having an alcoholic father embarrassed me, how him not working regularly, made it so that I couldn't have some of the things that other kids had. I blamed you for allowing it. But, as I got older, I thought more about you—how every attempt at a family vacation was a disaster, and about all the responsibilities you shouldered that should have been shared. What was your payoff? For all that you did for him, Mom, what did he do for you?"

"He loved me, Laura. He loved me just the way I was. I was beautiful to him, he made me believe that. It didn't matter to him that I couldn't lose the weight and that I would never even be a size fourteen. I was his girl. I was always his girl."

Could that really be enough? Should it be? To keep her by his side, and his family around him? Couldn't she see the consequences, or didn't they matter? It didn't seem possible that the loving words of a sweet drunk could negate unfulfilled dreams, or take the place of a real helpmate. What really was it that bonded a woman to a man, who for whatever reason never managed his disease, who allowed it to eat away his body until the woman he professed to love and the family he supposedly cherished was forced to watch him lose all hope, and finally his life?

Chapter Fifteen

The radio station played softly in the background as Laura traveled the stretch of moderately busy highway. The phone call from Terese shouldn't have surprised her, nor should the invitation to the fundraiser in Toledo. She hadn't severed all ties, or vowed not to see Terese again. Her mind, though, had settled into a sense of separation that included more than merely the distance of her physical move. More time with her mother and her new job, and longer times between calls had helped settle it there.

Yet, Laura surprised herself by accepting the invitation. The distance had made assessing their relationship easier, but it had been clear all along that it never fit into any conventional definition. It had consisted basically of a long chain of event appearances, accompanying Terese to more fundraisers than she could count, and culminating each night in a five-star hotel room. In between events there were expensive dinners, enjoyed before attending wonderful plays and musicals, and weekends spent at Terese's place. Two years and not a sign of a U-haul from either direction. "I miss you" spoken where "I love you" normally was. Unusual, to be sure.

She had decided not to decide whether she would stay the night. By nine o'clock, was all she had decided; she'd let her mother know by nine. Dinner would be over and the event just getting underway, a good time to break away and call.

ଓ ଓ ଓ

A "three-fork dinner" Sharon would have called it, a "500" in

Terese lingo. Designer silk and business attire. Not the highest-end fundraiser, but effective—less money per plate, more people attending. You assess the demographics and go with what works. The team had done its job, and the "face" of the team was still busy doing hers. Terese LaBraun was the name everyone knew and the one they trusted would put their money to good use.

Laura watched her work her magic right through dinner. Poised, and as impeccably dressed as the CEOs and socialites she solicited, 'T' LaBraun didn't waste a moment that could raise the contribution.

"I read a report recently," the man with the silver-gray hair sitting directly across from them began, "that said the biggest danger to the health of third-world children is the lack of safe water. What is United For Children doing on that front on a regular basis?"

"It's a huge problem, Don. UFC has people in several areas right now, working with local governments to put a plan in place. It has to be a coordinated effort, and it has to be a consistent treatment program. A hit and miss program just wouldn't be effective."

"And I imagine that involves a lot of red tape," he replied.

"It does. A few areas look very promising right now, and the plan is to keep a small monitoring team in place in each of those locales. But our largest concentration of personnel and resources right now is in Haiti. Eighty percent of the Haitian population is infected with intestinal parasites. And, according to the World Health Organization, those parasites eat up to twenty percent of a child's daily nutritional intake. Haiti is considered the second hungriest country in the world, so you can imagine the challenges that entails. And, I'm sure you can see how much we're counting on your extra help at this time."

"Absolutely," he said, then turned to the man on his right. "And I'll bet you'd be in for a little extra help, too, wouldn't you, Robert?"

The man nodded. "I like the idea of the monitoring teams.

I like knowing that my money gets where it is supposed to go."

"That's one of the things UFC prides itself on," Terese replied. "And the statistics you'll see tonight will show you just how much good your dollars are already doing in providing food and medicine for those kids."

And so it went—questions, conversation, commitments—charity centered, socialized business. No personal conversation with Terese, not until the entertainment begins. But Laura knew the protocol, it was her choice to be there. She could be included in this part of Terese's life, enjoying fine dinners and famous entertainers, or settle for random weeknights and non-event weekends. And, she also knew that, whatever her choice, Terese would be fine with it.

Laura checked her watch and excused herself from the table. She relaxed into a chair in a quiet end of the hallway and called her mother.

"Am I interrupting your movie?"

"I paused it. *Sister Act*. Did you see it?"

"I saw it when it came out years ago, and many times since. You'll love it. It's a real feel-good movie."

"Are you and Terese having a good night?"

"A lot of business talk, but nice. Hey, I just wanted to check on you. Did you get your medication okay?"

"All set. I'm gonna watch the rest of the movie and go to bed. You coming home tonight or tomorrow?"

"I'll be there when you get up in the morning, and I'm bringing you a surprise."

"Oh, you don't have to bring me anything. And it's okay if you want to stay. Just call me in the morning and let me know. It's time you get out and have a good time."

"Go watch your movie. And sing along, it'll make you feel like dancing."

A moment later, Terese appeared in the hallway with a welcoming smile and refreshment in either hand. "How's your mother?"

"Fine," Laura returned the smile, "watching *Sister Act*. I told her that I'm bringing her a surprise. So I purposely didn't tell her who is performing tonight."

"So she's a Hank Jones fan."

"Ever since I can remember, I heard the music of the Jones brothers. I brought along a CD. Would you have him sign it to her?"

"*You* can have him sign it. We'll go meet him afterwards."

"She is going to be thrilled."

As they settled once again at their table, Terese announced, "We have a dynamite program tonight. Jazz pianist Hank Jones is one of only a few musicians that the National Endowment for the Arts has named a Jazz Master." She acknowledged the smiles and raised eyebrows around the table, and continued. "We were so lucky to get him. When we saw that his schedule included a concert in Detroit this weekend, we contacted him right away. He graciously extended his stay one more day for us." Terese turned her attention to Laura and allowed her eyes to linger just a little longer, and her voice to lower to a more private tone. "It's nice to be able to share this with you. I'm glad you're here."

Laura smiled. "I am, too," she replied, enjoying what she knew was one of very few personal moments. Private time would come later, along with a decision about how much of that time would be right for tonight.

CR CS CR

Five-star or not, hotel rooms can do little to match a sense of home. Those things that define personal space and identify taste and personality—all missing. And now that she thought about it, Laura realized that Terese's condo was nearly as generic as this hotel room. Lots of neutral colors, furniture and accessories chosen by an interior designer—a budget-based, public-pleasing, ready-to-sell environment. No pieces with personal history or sentimental value. Even her home office would take only minutes to clear away any sign of actual use. Personal things were all tucked away and brought out only on rare occasion, and only when asked. Laura's request to see a photo album produced one filled with previous events—speakers and celebrities and places Terese had been—not at all what Laura had expected. She had to ask specifically for family photos, which Terese thought wouldn't be nearly as interesting to someone else.

So, here she was again, in another generic five-star hotel, wondering what that meant, not only personally, but to Terese.

They lounged comfortably on the love seat in the little sitting area of the suite. Terese slid her arm around Laura's shoulders and kissed the side of the face. "Did you enjoy the performance tonight?" she asked.

"It was very good. I'm still amazed at how many celebrities take the time to do events like this. There's not a lot of publicity in it for them—at least not what they're used to."

"And virtually no money," Terese added. "They're just good people giving back, paying forward . . . a lot like someone else I know," she said, adding another kiss. "Admirable."

"I don't know about admirable. When it's family, you do what you have to do."

"Yes, but of everyone in your family, you were the one who stepped up and made the sacrifices to take care of your mother."

"It's an unwritten rule, isn't it? Daughter, lesbian, unmarried, no kids—and in my case, throw physical therapist into the equation. I know my brothers and sister never gave it a second thought. Of course it would be me."

"What if you *had* been married with kids?"

"We would have made room for Mom."

Terese shifted around to face Laura. "See? To me that's an admirable decision."

"You don't think most women would inevitably make the same decision?"

"I hadn't even given it a serious thought until I knew about your situation. I realize that my family is atypical. But, even as an only child I would never be expected to care for either of my parents. They're both professionals, fiercely independent. They've always made decisions on their own—they don't even tell each other who they vote for in elections. There has been a financial plan in place for as long as I've been old enough to understand it, which will provide hired medical care for either or both of them in their home. I've never had that concern. I guess I never will."

"I wonder what I would do if I had that option."

"Oh, you might wonder, but you would make the same decision you made without options."

"You think that you know me that well?"

"One of the things that makes me good at what I do is the ability to make character judgments rather quickly. I've had a lot of time to get to know who you are."

And that was part of the attraction—that someone like Terese had known so much about her so early in their relationship and still maintained much of her own mystique. Without realizing it, Laura had offered up more and more about herself, unconsciously baiting those allusive bits and pieces that would flesh out the whole of Terese LaBraun. Not an even trade.

"I wasn't surprised at all," Terese was saying, "when you told me you were moving back to care for your mother. And, I'm not going to be surprised when you tell me that you're not staying tonight.

ଔ   ଔ   ଔ

It is entirely possible that some people are meant to live alone. The thought occurred two songs into Norah Jones's *Feels Like Home* CD, as Laura headed home. *A few lonely nights a week traded for the freedom to organize your own time and make decisions without compromise. Could it be explained that simply?*

She'd always thought that people living alone were lonely; that given the choice, the right opportunity, and the right person, they would naturally chose to live with someone. Yet, there was

Terese, seemingly content, happy in her space—alone. There was a lot to be said for it, she had to admit. No one to answer to, or argue with. No one to disappoint, except yourself.

In the years since Sharon, she had spent a lot of time alone, in her own space, adjusting. And it was somewhat scary at first—no one there to trust your fears to, no one to offer encouragement. Old friends had been alienated, and work associates were, well, work associates. So it took some time for evenings to lose the edginess, and even longer for the fibers of self-reliance to knit themselves securely around her. At first, she counted on the sounds of the television or the radio to fill the unbearable silence, their company needed late into the night until she could fall asleep. She wondered for a long time whether Sharon felt the same vulnerability.

Chapter Sixteen

"Let me ask you something, Sharon." Dr. Talbot had used their sessions well, to bring them methodically to this question. "Which sense of loss demands the most from you? The one that lies on the top layer of all that you've felt, the one you think is too sensitive to touch."

"How can I say one is more important than the others?"

"Not more important. The one you think you can't touch."

Sharon frowned. "If it's that sensitive, why do I want to touch it?"

"A logical assumption," the doctor admitted. "But, what happens to a flesh wound if you don't take care to clean and dress it?"

Sharon knew that the doctor was waiting for her to answer the obvious, one of the things that had become increasingly irritating during their sessions. She hadn't decided which was more annoying, the transparency of the doctor's method or the fact that it worked. "It gets infected," Sharon relented.

"Takes longer to heal, doesn't it? Probably makes things pretty uncomfortable meantime, right? Work, play—everything that touches it." She knew by now when not to wait for Sharon's acknowledgement. "It's really less painful, in the long run, to care for it early."

"I thought you said that we put things like that away until we're ready to deal with them."

"Ah, you were listening." The doctor offered an appreciative smile and continued. "But, when it is obviously festering, you need to start dealing with it, even if it's painful."

"I don't know how." Not exactly the truth. She knew the steps, they were the same ones that they had used to work through Donna and Evonne's deaths. But she was sure of what the doctor was aiming at, and they just didn't apply.

It was a waiting game—Sharon not ready to name it, Dr. Talbot not willing to drop it. Sharon fixed her focus on her favorite orange and black goldfish. She loved the smooth glides and quick turns, and the tail flowing gracefully behind.

"A divorce is a loss, too, Sharon. Can you say that you have mourned Laura yet?"

Mourned. No. You mourn death—the final, gone from this world, gone forever, end of life. She'd mourned her mother's death and her brother's, she'd mourned Donna and Evonne, and she'd mourned her childhood dog, Tigger. All gone forever. How could she mourn Laura?

"Not going through the grieving process is actually harder on your mind and body than going through it. It's a damaging stress that you can eliminate. We talked about this before."

"Dealing with my friend's deaths." The moment she heard the tone of her own words, Sharon knew that the doctor had heard the same thing. She had dug her heels in, braced her back against the corner.

"Whether you know it or not, you have been working very hard at keeping a tangle of emotions under the radar."

She knew.

"It's hard work."

She knew that, too.

"When was the last time you cried, Sharon?"

The question threw her for a moment. Her own answer surprised her. "The day after Laura moved."

Dr. Talbot raised her brows. "The last time you cried about anything?"

"The tears rolled a year ago when the ladder slipped and I landed across my back on a porch railing. Broke two ribs. I had muscle spasms for weeks that put me on my knees—literally, right down on the floor. Does that count?"

A grimace, and, "No, it's not the same thing. We're talking about a good emotional cry. Letting the sadness up and out. Letting yourself feel."

"So, I did that, right?"

"You think so?"

"Why do you always answer my questions with another question?"

A soft smile from the doctor. "Because you really know the answer better than I do."

"So, I'm paying you for the same reason that a guy who can swing a mean hammer hires a carpenter."

The doctor looked puzzled.

"He can hit the nail just as well as the carpenter, but the carpenter knows where to put the nail."

"Close enough," the doctor replied. "All right. I'll tell you what I think is going on and you tell me if you think I'm wrong."

"Earn your money, Doc."

A light laugh and a raise of her brows, then the doctor replied, "I plan to do just that. So, here we go. Losing someone to a divorce, or from a long-term relationship, is many times more difficult to grieve because it doesn't seem as final as the death of someone you love. There's often a period of on-again/off-again, and love/hate that delays a feeling of finality. And, for the partner who did not initiate the split, there's often a lingering sense of hope that she and her partner will get back together."

Sharon shifted position in her chair and broke eye contact to focus again on her fish.

The significance wasn't lost on the doctor. "That's why every time anger threatens your hope, you skip on by and try to strike a bargain—if you do this, or accomplish that, then she'll come back. But when that doesn't happen, you are wide open for depression to take over. Although you are essentially jumping around in the middle of the process, I think you are still in full denial."

Sharon's eyes shot back to meet the doctor's.

"Am I wrong?"

No intention. She has no intention. The message couldn't have been more clear. Yet, even then, didn't I try to bargain? Refuse to accept, drop into depression?

Sharon leaned forward on her knees and dropped her head.

"You can't be angry at her if you want her back, can you, Sharon?"

Sharon shook her head but refused to raise it. "I can't be angry at her because it wasn't her fault. It was mine."

"Let's assume that that's true, and while we're at it, we'll assume that Laura believes it is, too. What's keeping you from accepting the result and moving on?"

"Doesn't dating someone for the past seven months count as moving on?"

"I can't answer that for you."

Of course not. Spoon-feeding is for wimps.

"I *can* tell you that you have to be able to identify each layer before you can peel it away. If you ignore a layer, it will block you from getting beyond it . . . I can't get you beyond that sensitive place until you're ready to deal with the pain."

Chapter Seventeen

When did Friday become just another day? Just a day like any other workday, starting early, ending late, with only the promise of another workday to follow in the morning.

Sharon's truck bounced from pothole to pothole, now too numerous to avoid. Oakwood Street still clung to the bottom of the road commission's priority list. The holes would probably be filled just in time for them to be covered in five inches of snow again. Meantime, Sharon's back would suffer the jolts until she turned for home on Willow. Evidently, there was a demarcation line between Willow's early spring maintenance and Oakwood's none. It was only natural, then, that everyone was tempted to make up the time on Willow that they had lost on the rougher streets. The muscles of her back relaxed and Sharon welcomed the relief that would last only until morning.

For too long now she'd been longing for that TGIF exhilaration. Jumping into the day with unwarranted energy, smiling through the day with thoughts of a night of laughter and mischief and friends. No worries, no stress. Weekends of sound sleep, late into the mornings, and riding and four-wheeling, and ball games. *Was it really that long ago—that last day that they were all together four-wheeling on Donna and Evonne's land? The day bright and sunny, the trails a challenge of hills and woods and mud and water. And the laughter—tear-streaking, side-aching laughter that rivaled any she could remember.*

Everyone knew the rules: arms and legs covered, always a helmet, keep a three-vehicle distance, make sure the rider ahead of you clears a hill before you climb, and always leave the tank full at the end of the day. Important rules for the obvious reasons, and for the not so obvious.

Sharon knew the trails better than most and led the way through the wooded terrain. Deanne, not so familiar, followed Sharon. They maneuvered their machines into the cool, moist air of the woods, crept over exposed roots, zipped around trees, and climbed in and out of ravines. They were deep in the woods, all rules intact, until Deanne made an assumption she shouldn't have. Sharon disappeared over the bank of a ravine, and without waiting until Sharon had successfully climbed the opposite side, Deanne rode over and down the bank. It was only then that she realized that Sharon was stopped in a foot of black muck at the base of the opposite bank. Before Deanne could attempt a yell over the rumble of the engines, Sharon gunned her accelerator, the huge tires spun their way through the muck and up the bank, and Deanne was covered from head to toe in black muck.

A short distance down the trail, Sharon stopped and turned to see if Deanne had made it across and nearly fell off her seat in laughter. It didn't matter that no one believed that it was unintentional, the laughter was worth all the accusations. Remembering it, even now, brought a much-needed chuckle. How she would love to have those weekends back, she thought, as she pulled into her drive.

The sun setting so late in the day now made it seem earlier than it was, but her body knew it had been a long day. She had just decided to cancel with Kim tonight when the sound of a truck brought her attention to the road—an older blue pick-up from a few blocks down coming home from work.

As she stepped from the truck, she caught movement out of the corner of her eye that startled her. "No," she yelled, as Hank's little dog dashed to the road. "No, no," she screamed, waving her arms frantically at the driver. But he sat too high up to see something that close.

Sharon raced into the road as the right tire hit the dog and sent her spinning beneath the truck. Her words softened into cries. "No, oh no. Please God."

The truck skidded to a stop and the driver, dressed in work jeans and baseball cap, jumped out. "What? What happened?" He rushed behind the truck where Sharon was kneeling. "Oh, Jesus. I didn't see him. I'm so sorry." He leaned over Sharon. She was stroking the little dog, who was still moving and crying.

He rushed back to the cab and grabbed an old gray hoodie and hurried back to Sharon. "Here, wrap him up and jump in the truck. Where is your vet hospital?"

Without hesitation Sharon slid her hands under the little body, wrapped the sweatshirt snuggly, and climbed quickly into the truck. It took a moment, though, to think. Adrenaline made her voice shake. "I don't have a vet. If you know where the nearest one is, just go. Hurry, please," she pleaded.

He turned the corner without a stop and stepped on the gas. "We're on our way. How's he doing?"

Sharon held the dog to her chest and kissed her head. "I don't know," she replied. "I should have fixed that damn fence. Got the stuff right in the back of my truck . . . I'm sorry, girl. What's wrong with me?" Tears made their way down her face onto the sweatshirt. Sharon pressed her cheek to the downy little head and cried silently.

"Jesus, I'm sorry. I'm so sorry." Danny McCarty drove his pick-up as though his own life depended on how quickly he reached the hospital. He slowed down close to the speed limit only for traffic, and blew through stop signs. He concentrated on driving and limited his comments to an occasional, "It'll be okay" and "We're almost there."

The moment that they squealed up to the emergency entrance everything became a blur of activity—a gentle handoff, a flurry of questions, and people rushing down the hallway. Then, as if the centrifugal force of a merry-go-round had thrown her off standing up, she found herself in a dizzy fog in the waiting room with Danny McCarty. He had evidently just introduced himself and was waiting for her reply.

"Sharon . . . Davis," she said and dropped to the nearest chair to try to stop the lightheadedness.

Cap in his hands, and blue eyes surrounded in creased concern, he said, "I'm sorry about your dog. I want to help pay for the medical expenses."

"She's not mine. Well, she should be, but she belongs to the old man across the street . . . I . . . I guess I should call him."

"Oh. Then tell him that I want to help. I'll pay whatever I can."

Sharon nodded and searched her phone for the number. She let it ring a long time, and Hank finally picked up. "Hank, it's Sharon from across the street," she began. Then, with the shakiness back in her voice, she explained what happened and where she was.

Danny had walked to the large wall of windows out of earshot, so when he returned, Sharon explained. "He said to let her go, he's got no money to pay for the medical."

"You told him that I'd help?"

Sharon nodded. "I guess she's mine now if she makes it. It won't be cheap."

"Yeah. My Lab went through cancer surgery two years ago. But he's the best damn dog. I couldn't put him down without giving him a chance."

"He made it?"

"He'll be waitin' with his Frisbee in his mouth as soon as I get home."

Sharon smiled and nodded. She stood again, trying to calm the nerves making her stomach quiver. She walked to the empty reception counter, saw no movement in the hallway, and returned. "Do you think she has a chance? She's so tiny."

"If she's got a chance, this is the place to be. I wish I had Dr. Meredith for my own doctor."

His words gave her a moment of hopefulness, but the emergence of a slight woman in a white coat sent a stab of fear through her midsection.

Clasping a clipboard to her chest, she extended her other hand to both Danny and Sharon, and spoke in a quiet, serious tone. "I'm

Dr. Meredith. I know you are very concerned, so I'm going to get right to it. She has internal bleeding and we need to operate immediately if we are going to have a chance to save her."

Sharon was already nodding.

"I want you to know that it will be costly and we won't know the extent of her injuries until we get in to take a look. And, there is no guarantee that she will make it through surgery. You need to decide right now whether to put her to sleep or try to save her."

Sharon didn't even look to Danny. It didn't matter if she ended up with the entire cost. "Do I need to sign a form? I want you to do everything you can to save her."

The doctor nodded, handed her the clipboard, and pointed to the line needing a signature.

Sharon scribbled her name and Dr. Meredith squeezed her arm. "We'll do everything we can," she said, before hurrying down the hall.

Then that was that—another life left to fate, out of Sharon's hands, nothing left to do except sit and wait and hope. She let go of the back end of a breath that she was unaware she'd been holding.

"I'll wait with you," he was saying—right out there, with compassion displayed as unabashedly as the company logo on his sweat-stained T-shirt. Sharon clamped onto it; using it, needing its support.

"I'll call someone for a ride later. You don't have to stay," she replied despite wanting him to stay in the worst way.

"No, this is the miserable part," he said, shaking his head. "You just sit here, waitin' and hopin' for the best and dreadin' that it'll be the worst. I know how it was when Bear was in surgery. If I wasn't here, I'd be thinking about it anyway."

And so they waited, together, and talked; about Bear and the undisputable bond between human and dog. "He forgives me for being late from work the second he sees the truck." Danny occupied the chair next to her, more relaxed now, a work boot resting on his knee. "My ex wasn't so understanding. We're better friends now that we don't live together."

She waited for the inevitable personal questions, but they never came. Whether it was an innate sensitivity not to pry, or a natural acceptance of the obvious, didn't matter. He made her comfortable. He made her think of Ronnie.

He told her about work, and last winter's layoffs, and taking Bear with him to Kansas to roof houses. About towns building houses as fast as they could to house the rush of people to a resurgence of work in the mines. About clean coal and renewable energy. And why he came back. "The wind is like nothing I've ever seen. One minute you're up there, and the sweat is rolling down your sides and the air is so still, and the next minute there's a gust of wind that hits you so fast that you're spread-eagle just trying to stay on the roof. One of the most dangerous jobs out there, but the pay was incredible."

"Would you go back?"

He thought for a second. "I guess—as long as I wasn't married, I probably would. I gotta work somewhere. It's good money, you can't argue with that, but it's a widow-maker."

His hand gripped and released the bend of his knee. Strong and thickly veined—hardworking like her own. She realized that she hoped he didn't have to go back. Then, his hand was on her arm, and Dr. Meredith was approaching.

They stood. Sharon tried to read the doctor's expression, grasped unsuccessfully for immediate relief.

The doctor's eyes were dark and round beneath a gently creased tent of sincerity. She locked them now onto Sharon's as she stepped forward. "She made it through surgery," she said in a cautionary tone.

Sharon withheld relief.

"She has external stitches and a lot of internal stitches and broken ribs and a broken leg. The impact seems to have been a glancing blow to the rear of her body, and we didn't see any injury to her head. That's the good news. We need to watch her closely for the next twenty-four hours, and after that the concern will be keeping her still long enough for the bones to heal correctly."

It was a tone that Danny recognized. "You're hopeful."

"Yes," the doctor nodded, "hopeful. We'll take very good care of her. Staff will watch her closely tonight, and I'll give one or both of you a call first thing in the morning."

"Can I see her?" Sharon asked.

"Of course," she replied. "Of course."

"I'll call a friend for a ride, Danny. You don't have to wait for me. If you give me your number, I'll keep you updated."

"You're sure?" he asked with a hand on her shoulder.

Sharon nodded. "Thanks, Danny. I really appreciated you staying with me."

෬ ෫ ෬

The small room, with its wall of windows on the hallway, was dimly lit and quiet. Built-in stainless steel cages filled another wall. All the cages were empty except for the one right in the middle at eye level. There she was, wrapped snuggly in a white towel, with only her head visible.

"She'll be coming out of the anesthesia gradually. We'll keep her in here by herself so she won't be stressed, and our emergency night staff will monitor her . . . Go ahead, you can open the cage."

Sharon opened the door and gently stroked the dog's head. "She's shivering," she said, cupping the little head in her hand.

"It's a normal reaction to the anesthesia. For some reason they quiver as they begin coming out of it."

"Would it hurt her if I held her?"

"You can hold her. Her back leg and hip are broken and she has two broken ribs—"

"Ohh," Sharon said with a grimace, "I know that pain."

"Well, she's casted and her chest banded, and we'll keep her medicated for pain. You won't hurt her. Here." Dr. Meredith

90

lifted her patient carefully and placed the bundle in Sharon's arms. "I'll be right back with a chair."

Through the towel, Sharon could feel the rigid cast, and intermittent quivering. She cradled the bundle gently and pressed her lips to the dog's head. The familiar smell of her hair was tinged with a strong scent of antiseptic. She held her close, the little head tucked against her cheek, hoping that the warmth of her body would help stop the quivering.

Soft whimpering sounds brought Sharon to tears. She'd held them at bay until now, but without Danny, without the diversion of their conversation, she was helpless to stop them. "Shh," she whispered, tears soaking into the towel, "it's gonna to be okay, little girl. It's gonna be okay."

Sharon paced a small circle around the room trying to gain composure, but the door opened before she could. Dr. Meredith rolled a chair into the room ahead of her, and looked up to meet Sharon's eyes.

"Oh, yes, it's hard," she said. "It's hard to see her like this. Here, sit down . . . I know this is hard."

"I'm sorry," Sharon replied, not wanting to move her arm away to wipe the tears. "I don't cry like this. I'm sorry."

The doctor placed both hands on Sharon's arm and knelt beside the chair. "You can stay here with her for as long as you want."

The soft sounds of whimpering began again. "Is she crying?" Sharon asked.

"No, the sounds are results from involuntary movement of muscles, like what causes the quivering. She's still out, and the pain medication is going to keep her comfortable."

Sharon tried to blink away the blurriness.

"We'll see how she does. We'll know tomorrow."

Sharon nodded. "I guess she's mine now. I'll take care of her if . . ." Tears welled again. "She doesn't even have a name. I can't give her a name if . . . I just can't."

Dr. Meredith squeezed Sharon's arm. "I think you should give her a name."

She had fallen asleep in a time cocoon. No visible clocks, no sound, no movement. Gail from the night staff brought her rolled towels as a pillow behind her head, and routinely checked on her patient, but for most of the night Sharon slept with her new responsibility in her arms.

When the door opened again, Sharon woke to a smiling Dr. Meredith entering the room. "Gail said that you spent the night. What a good mother you are," she said, then immediately focused on the bundle in Sharon's arms. "Oh, and look at the ears perk up."

Sharon shifted stiffly upright. Yes, the ears were up. The big brown eyes looking right at her. "Ohh, that's my girl," she said softly. "Oh, yeah. She looks good, Doctor. Doesn't she look good?"

"She's a little trooper." Dr. Meredith leaned in for a closer look. "Have you given your little trooper a name yet?"

"Part of the night I was dreaming," Sharon replied, as the doctor lifted her patient. "And, in my dream I was calling her Abby."

"I think that's a perfect name."

"I don't know where it came from."

"Well, it's in the right place now, isn't it, Abby? Let's go see how everything looks this morning."

The exhilarating sense of relief lasted until Abby was unwrapped in the examining room. Sharon was unprepared for the sight of the broken little body. With the towel pulled away, the cast, the strapping, and the bloody stitches brought home the severity of Abby's injuries. Sharon closed her eyes and took a deep breath in an attempt to quell the sickness she felt in her stomach. Only minutes ago she was ready to take Abby home, confident in her own ability to care for her, sure that she would be better off there. Now, though, she wanted every bit of magic that the doctor's hands could impart. It didn't matter what the cost, or how much time it took, she just wanted Abby well. Tears welled again and Sharon tried to wipe them clear as Dr. Meredith looked up.

"I know," the doctor said softly. "It's hard to see. But, she's really doing well."

More tears, wiped quickly. "How can something so small make your heart feel like it's going to explode?"

"You know," the doctor replied, "love just doesn't have anything to do with size." She covered Sharon's hand, which was gripping the edge of the stainless table, with her own. "And, even though it feels like it, our hearts won't explode. They'll just expand as much as they have to in order to take it all in."

"Yeah." Sharon nodded vigorously and stroked Abby's head.

"So, let's talk about how we can help Abby."

"I hope I can take good care of her. I want to make sure she gets whatever she needs."

"I'm not worried about that. If love alone could heal, you would have healed her by now."

Chapter Eighteen

No Saturdays off, especially now. Understood. Asking for a Saturday off would have to mean the difference between life and death, but thanks to Dr. Meredith that concern had been eased. Leaving Abby in her care for as long as needed felt like the right thing to do.

Danny thought so, too. In that tone of calm reassurance that had helped Sharon through the worst of yesterday, he reassured her once again. Part of his lunch break would be spent checking on Abby. Today will be a much better day.

Kasey picked her up from the hospital and listened to an emotional but relieved Sharon relive the night before. Her words, although they defined the positive, did nothing to divert the initial sense of dread. That all too familiar fear that shot normal days full of black holes—dropping you free-falling through the unknown, and daring you to stand when your feet hit the bottom. Too many of those days for Sharon, too many days free-falling right beside her. Yesterday, though, Kasey reminded herself, had been different. So, today she listened gratefully.

The blame was shouldered realistically. "God, Kasey, if I had only dragged my ass over there and dug in that trench and buried that chicken wire. I had that roll right in the back of the truck all week." And the claim for the blame, mentioned only twice all day long—owning the lack of priority without obsession.

"I tried to get the vision out of my head, Kase. It was horrible. I was so sure that she was dead. And when I picked her up and she looked at me, I didn't want to let go of her. I tried so hard not to think about her dying, and Danny kept talking, and it helped."

They sat in the truck, in the driveway; no attempt to leave it, no rush to begin work. And Kasey wondered when it was that she had tired of talking. It wasn't a conscious decision, the one that deprived Sharon of diversional chatter. It wasn't intentional.

"I was so glad they let me stay all night and hold her. I think she knew I was holding her. Do you think it helped her? You know, she was quivering so much."

"Of course it helped. You kept her warm and made her feel secure, even if she didn't know it was you until she woke up. She's going to be one happy little pup to see you picking her up. She doesn't know it yet, but she is done having to dig tunnels to come play with her favorite human. What time do we need to pick her up?"

"Before six, but you don't have to cart me around. Take me home to get my truck when we break for lunch."

"No, I've got a little bed that the girls refuse to use, so we'll swing by and get that. Then you're going to have to pick up food for her, and chewies. And, I know you'll be tempted to hold her while you're trying to drive . . . Besides, we have to get the kitchen put back together today. That could mean working through lunch."

ᏇᎦ ᏇᎦ ᏇᎦ

It was as if she had become the parent of a newborn. The soft-sided bed Kasey had given her was only the beginning. The amount of stuff necessary for Abby's care was staggering. She left the store with wee pads and baby shampoo and doggie tooth-paste and nail clippers. And she left the animal hospital with pain medication and antibiotic and antiseptic and oral syringes—and a schedule now built around a small ball of helplessness. Satur-day night, with Dr. Meredith's instructions taped to the kitchen cupboard, Sharon began the process of adjusting her life.

ᏇᎦ ᏇᎦ ᏇᎦ

She woke early and turned off her alarm minutes before the 6 a.m.

set time, and checked for the umpteenth time to be sure Abby, in her little bed right next to Sharon's pillow, was indeed all right. She hadn't moved much at all and, as Dr. Meredith predicted, slept all night.

Sharon left the bed carefully and tried to stretch the stiffness from her body on the way to the kitchen. She retrieved Abby's medicine from the refrigerator, and blinked the blur from her eyes. She shook the bottle, retracted the designated milligrams with the syringe, and padded back to the bedroom.

Thank God the visions of forcing pills down a resistant dog's throat were unfounded. Sharon greeted Abby, awake and resting her chin on the soft side of her bed, and quickly squirted the medicine into the side of her mouth. "There, baby girl, right on time. We're not going to let you hurt."

She picked her up, bed and all, and carried her to the kitchen. "Okay, here you go," she said, placing the bed on the floor by the table. "Breakfast is coming right up. You're getting exactly what the doctor feeds her dogs. What do you think about that?"

Despite being exhausted, she had cooked up the chicken breast and rice last night—a smart decision. Now she warmed up a portion for Abby, and added an egg to the rest for herself. She checked the clock. "Twenty minutes, Abbs, and then we're gonna have to try standing long enough for a bathroom break."

Her apprehension, her self-doubt, diminished as the day wore on. She could do this. Meds every six hours with food, potty breaks, keep the incision clean, and lots of love. The absolute best medicine according to Dr. Meredith.

And Danny was so right. What a blessing it would be to have a doctor who cared as much about their human patients as Dr. Meredith did her four-legged ones. A Sunday morning call to check on Abby was totally unexpected. Was she eating, standing long enough to go to the bathroom, sleeping comfortably? The evening call placed her in line for sainthood. Expect Abby to become more active after tomorrow. Keep her as quiet as possible. Watch her stitches. Be sure to call if there are any questions.

Sharon settled Abby back in her dog bed after the last trip outside, and cradled it in her lap in front of the desk. Three days worth of e-mails and Facebook notifications filled her inbox.

"Well, damn, Abbs, the world kept right on goin' without us." Abby lifted her head and began licking the bottom of Sharon's arm. "Yeah, I know, if you can't eat it, or chase it, or lick it, what good is e-mail?"

Chapter Nineteen

Admittedly, Kasey's expectations the first day Sharon brought Abby to work with her were less than enthusiastic. Caring for an injured pet, with specific needs and added worries, was difficult enough under normal circumstances. Plop that care right in the middle of a construction zone, though, with its dust and fumes and noise, and it hardly seemed workable. Yet, Sharon made it work. In fact, for the past seven days, she'd made it surprisingly enjoyable.

Can you fall in love in five minutes? You can when a little pup pushes herself up, broken and patched, to greet you with a fervor of kisses. It was a quick fall for Kasey—less than five minutes really, for all those concerns and worries about safety and wasted time to vanish. Sharon had it all covered—medicine, precooked food, Abby's bed; and she tucked her safely in the first floor bedroom. Perfect. And the strictly adhered to, by-the-clock schedule was, well, notable.

So, this morning, Sharon's truck, already parked and unloaded in the drive, was no surprise. The unexpected was Sharon, kneeling in the bathroom and up to her elbows in thin set.

"What are you doing?" Kasey asked. "I thought you were going to be in Lansing. Did the protest march get postponed?"

"No," Sharon pushed a floor tile into place and wiped the edge clean with her finger. "I decided not to go."

A bit of disbelief, maybe the size of Texas. "Sharon, I can take good care of Abby. I know your schedule by heart by now, and I have your instructions and the doctor's number right here. We'll be fine."

"We need to get this house listed. I can get the tile laid today."

"Take the day, Sharon. We'll get it done this week."

A resolute shake of her head. "I'm more needed here."

Unwilling to be left out any longer, Abby hobbled down the hall and rested against Sharon's leg.

Needed—yes. Wanted—of course. But "I'm not planning any guilt trip, Sharon. I know how important this is to you. So, if you need to be there, you go."

She held Abby now, who was stretching up and aiming an errant tongue at Sharon's chin. "We've got everything so well-organized. The word's been out to all the blogs and Facebook for weeks now. It's being tweeted everywhere. Our whole group will be there, and a huge group from Detroit. They're coming from all over the state. Sage and Deanne are even marching."

"Jenny, too?"

Sharon nodded. "Took the day off work. She'll call and let me know how it's going. There's nothing else to be done. Just my body there or not there."

"You're sure?"

"Yeah . . . I'm gonna move Abby's bed here in the doorway. She cries now if I shut the bedroom door, and she'll hobble down here again if I don't." She squeezed the top of Kasey's shoulder. "Let's kick ass on this house."

ೞ ೞ ೞ

And kick ass they did. With twenty-something energy and forty-something skills, they painted and tiled as if they could close a sale tomorrow. Unrealistic, but the feeling was intoxicating.

Sharon hummed an accompaniment to the song Kasey sang as it drifted through the bathroom window, and dropped another tile into place. She loved the sound of Kasey's voice, pitch-perfect, pure and natural. It coaxed her own hesitant sound to catch a ride on the strength of Kasey's notes. Pitiful on its own, Sharon's voice sounded almost acceptable in unison.

The tile was more than half laid when the phone rang. The news begged to be shared. "Kase," she called through the window, "the media's all over it."

Kasey moved along the pick to peer in. "Jenny?"

"Yep, they interviewed her and a spokesman from Equality Michigan. They are all over it."

"This might even make the national news."

"I'm thinking so. Jenny sounded relieved. She didn't want to be the one talking to the media, but who better?"

"Exactly. Laws need faces. Put a personal face on this, because it is personal."

"It got their attention, that's for sure. So many people showed up that it forced a response from the governor's office."

"What did they say?"

"Only that the governor has a lot on her plate right now, and that she will take the matter under consideration. But, it did get their attention. They know that this is not a decision to be taken lightly."

"A high five to you, my friend. Job well done."

ය ౪ ය

The last of the tiles had been cut, the buzz of the wet saw quieted. Kasey inched along the end of the pick to finish painting the house trim. Minutes later, Sharon emerged from the back door with a squirming Abby in her arms.

"Potty break," she announced, releasing her in the grass and watching her hobble into the best squat she could manage. "It's a heck of a way to be housebroken, eh, little girl?"

"I can't believe how much better she's doing." Kasey rested the paintbrush on the edge of the can and climbed down. "She'd be trying to run if it wasn't for that cast."

"Yeah, I don't think I could have kept her from breaking her stitches. The pain meds make her feel better than she is."

Kasey knelt beside a wiggling, anxious Abby. "Such a different energy than cats. My girls are way too cool to wiggle. I swear she's going to wag herself right off her feet."

Sharon offered a relieved smile. "She has no clue how bad it really was."

"A blessing I would bet a lot of people wish they had." *A blessing she wished Sharon had. But, that was impossible. No one past that magical age of innocence could have such a blessing. Unless they were ignorant—and really, at times, there is a lot to be said for a good old case of ignorance. What you don't know can't hurt you? Hmm, if only.*

"She may not know that you saved her life, but she has to know that you are taking very good care of her."

"For once I've actually done something that made a difference."

Yes, something, anything . . . everything, to avoid another death, another loss on her watch. "You *have* made a real difference, and not just with Abby . . . You have to start enjoying the now moments in your life."

Abby managed to stand up and get both front feet on Kasey's knee. *Irresistible.* Kasey picked her up and nuzzled the soft face. "You sure picked a cute one."

Sharon shook her head. "I didn't, Kase. She picked me."

Chapter Twenty

Changes are impossible to see this late at night. Surely there would be changes. Laura took her foot off the accelerator and, two houses down from Sharon's, let the car find it's own speed. She turned down the radio, but had no idea why.

It was still Sharon's house, she knew from the last card her mother received. The car rolled closer and something made her heart pound harder. *Fear. Just fear of Sharon seeing her, fear of looking like a fool.*

A blue truck was parked in the drive. *Still a blue truck.* A light shone from the front bedroom window. *What's to fear? She doesn't know this car, or have any reason to look out the window.*

The streetlight behind her was out, the one ahead shone a pale glow that crept over a Honda parked on the street, and reached across the familiar front yard to the porch. Her porch—once. Her yard, her garden, her life. She could still feel herself here—morning coffee on the porch, the sound of birds welcoming the day, the smell of nature warming with the sun. Sounds and smells missed in the apartments, missed in her life. And missed even more, the sharing of them. Early mornings with Sharon, sharing their plans for the day, upbeat with new energy. Late summer nights, her favorite time, filled with stories and easy laughter. Relaxed, de-stressed, she loved that time. She needed that time with Sharon. And when it was gone, long before she left, an important part of the intimacy was gone as well. That, too, like the sounds and smells, had never been replaced. And probably never would be.

Laura breathed the familiar scents wafting through the open window, and for a moment she was home. Anxious for the sight of Sharon's smile, anxious to hug her tightly, and to listen to the story of the day. Sometimes it was an accident, more embarrassing than painful, that should have been taped and sent to AFV. Often it was a pitifully unavoidable story involving their least favorite inspector. Funny that her next thought was whether they still have to endure old Larry the Lush's questionable and frustrating inspections.

She was staring at the house when the bedroom light went out, and Laura quickly realized that she had been sitting behind the Honda that was parked in front of the house. Her focus turned immediately to the street. She pulled out from behind the car and accelerated down the block to the stop sign before finally exhaling. Once around the corner, she pulled the car next to the curb and stopped.

What would have been next? If that car hadn't been parked out front? If the bedroom light hadn't gone out and the connection made? What would I have done, let selfishness sweep away the guilt?

I wouldn't have made it to the door. Couldn't have stood there, chancing what I would see on her face, in her eyes—chancing what I would feel, what she would feel. What made me think I could? That I care about her, worry that she is okay? Isn't it really only about me—my feelings, my curiosity? Selfish, horribly selfish.

I can't do this again. I won't do this again.

Chapter Twenty-One

Kasey rubbed the caulk from her hands over the trash can in the kitchen. "Caulking's done," she called toward the doorway. "This sucker's getting listed tomorrow." She washed in the sink and dried her hands on the way down the hall.

"How's the bathroom coming?" she asked, bending to pick up Abby.

Sharon, working on her hands and knees, spoke as she backed through the doorway. "Last coat of sealer on the grout. Five minutes and I'm done."

"It looks good. Clean, neutral. Medium-colored grout, good choice."

"I'm psyched up now to get my own bathroom finished. I started it yesterday when I got home. I love the color of this grout. Do you mind if I use the leftover at home?"

"Of course not."

"I just wanted to be sure that we didn't need it somewhere else. I'll save some out for repairs."

"Hopefully, we won't own this house when it needs repair. We can afford to give it a month before we resort to renting it. It's priced right, so let's hope it sells quickly."

Sharon sat back on her heels and blew out an exhale that puffed her cheeks. "Done."

"It looks—"

"Hello?" The voice called in from the front door. "Hey, Sharon?"

"In the hall, Kim. Come on in . . . Hey," Sharon greeted as Kim rounded the corner, "you're just in time for lunch."

But, Kim's expression was far from appetizing. She spoke directly to Sharon. "Can I talk to you for a few minutes?"

"I'll take Abby out," Kasey said, excusing herself from the hallway. "Good to see you, Kim."

Sharon stood and began. "I'm sorry I haven't—"

"I don't need 'sorry'." Her stance, weight on one foot, hands in the back pockets of her jeans, nearly shouted aggravation.

"An explanation then?"

Stoic blue-green.

Sharon pressed on. "You did tell me to let you know when Abby was better and things had calmed down."

"Three weeks ago."

"I've been really busy, Kim. But I wouldn't have kicked you out if you'd stopped over."

"I drove by the night before last."

"Why didn't you stop?"

"You're joking, right? One of your humor bites that slid right off the scale this time."

Okay, keep your mouth shut and think. What the hell is she talking about. The night before . . . I got nothing. Sharon furled her brow and shook her head. "Hey, admonish me when I deserve it—I'll take it like a woman. But—"

Kim turned to leave, but abruptly turned back. "You can't even be honest and leave me with a shred of respect for you. I guess I expected too much from you." This time she turned and didn't look back.

"Kim," Sharon called to her back, "I really have no idea . . ." But it wasted effort.

Long, swift strides had Kim already down the front walk, and headed for her Jeep.

For a few puzzling moments Sharon didn't move. It seemed clear, she knew exactly what she was doing that day, that night—in fact, every day and night for weeks. So, what was she missing?

Still searching for the missing piece, Sharon dropped onto the back step next to Kasey. How quickly the exhilaration of the mornings' accomplishments had dissolved.

Abby's lopsided attempts at a run had Kasey laughing.

"You laughing at my poor little drunken sailor?"

"I am," Kasey replied. "I think she's trying to entertain me—and she's doing a great job."

Sharon nodded absently.

"Everything okay?" Kasey asked.

Her brows knit together tightly above her nose. "I guess not."

"You guess?"

"Well, Kim's totally pissed and I'm supposed to know why."

"She's seeing smoke that isn't there?"

"No fire, no smoke . . . I knew she was getting impatient because I was staying home. The time she spent at the house turned into phone calls, then those turned into text messages. Then those got downright anemic . . . She's no homebody, but I knew that."

"Maybe she's jealous of your new girl here."

"No, she knew I had to take care of her."

Kasey picked up the end of the piece of rope that Abby kept dropping in front of her and played tug of war. "Did it cut into your social time?"

"Yeah."

"Did it cut into your intimate time?"

No answer.

"I'm guessing that Abby's bed is still up on your bed, and that there hasn't been a whole lot of sex happening . . . yeah?"

"You gonna tell me that nothing ever takes priority over your sex life?"

"Sure, things take priority. Sometimes even things that shouldn't. But Connie's not fourteen and we've been doing this for a while."

Silence.

"I'm just saying that Kim's expectations are different," Kasey added.

A revelation? Hardly. One of the dead ends that Kim prided herself on identifying? Probably.

"We had her expectations once, didn't me?"

"I can't remember," Kasey said with a laugh.

Chapter Twenty-Two

Saturday felt very much like a day at camp—a perfect cap to a week-long summer visit from Sage's sister Cimmie and her daughter, Naline.

The morning began with Deanne and Cimmie packing the days' rations, and Sage and the girls mapping out the schedule. Backpacks fully stocked, the troop of five began their trek around the lake.

They decided to hike the south end of the lake early, before the sun was high over the open terrain. That way, they would be in the woods on the north end during the hottest part of the day. A long haul for the girls; but they had been asking to do this since last summer, so no one had the heart to say no again. Besides, there was more to be gained than merely the fun of the challenge.

Inexpensive cameras and keen little eyes captured close-ups of bugs and butterflies and not-so-close shots of deer and birds and squirrels. They collected leaves of the different plants and trees and pressed them between the pages of small notebooks they carried in their packs. Later they would look them up and identify them. The girls were most excited, though, to reach each of the landmarks that they had heard Deanne's niece talk so much about. And their spacing around the lake made them perfect stopping points to rest and eat.

The sun had begun to warm the edge of the field as they found the twin cypress trees and the opening to the path that would lead them closer to the edge of the water—and the rock.

"How much further, Nu' ye?"

"Is it as big as Beano said? She said it's as big as a car."

"Just up here," Sage replied, "and you can see for yourself." Sage turned to Cimmie. "Deanne's niece has told them so many stories about the rock, and the things they are going to see today. I'm sure they have some fantasy-sized visions in their heads."

A few yards farther and Sage turned right around the weeping branches of a dogwood, then stepped to the side.

The girls squealed in unison, and ran past Sage to the rock.

Cimmie followed close behind. "Wow, now that's a rock." She marveled with the girls, who were walking around the large curved mass, running their hands over the smooth, warm surface. "Look at the colors. It's beautiful."

Deanne slipped her arm around Sage's waist and spoke softly. "And full of secrets we'll keep to ourselves."

Some, Sage thought with a smile. Secrets and memories that lit an inner glow. The heat of new love, exposed, played out on earth's very core. The grip of love, the endure-until-death love that she had thought impossible, held there in the perfect Rubenesque curve of the rock. Mother Earth's proof of forever, cradling her in love's same promise. And now there were new promises, of love beyond the flesh, and introductions to lessons that must be passed on.

So, together they all took a much-needed break, exploring the rock, climbing and playing and talking. And when they were rested, they set off on the trail to find the next special place.

As planned, they found it in the heat of the day, tucked deep in the thickest part of the woods. Tumbling between moss-covered rocks was a crystal clear, spring-fed waterfall. Above it, intersecting branches of ancient maples formed an arbor that kept the air as cool as air conditioning. Within minutes the girls had shed their shoes and socks and were giggling knee-deep in an icy pool of water at the base of the little falls. Welcoming the relief, the adults soon followed. They splashed and played and laughed, and then, once again refreshed, they moved on. A quick stop at a modern version of an outhouse, and they were off to the great tree.

Throughout the day, the focus had been on the girls—safely wrapping their lessons of nature in hours of fun and adventure. Most importantly, it was a block of time for them to learn together. There hadn't been a time when the girls had much more than a week here, and a week there, shuffling between New York and Michigan for birthdays and holidays and time together. And until Cimmie or Jeff could find the right job opportunity in Michigan, frequent travel would remain the only solution.

Now, with the girls busy climbing the low gnarly branches of the great oak, the women settled into conversation.

"Have you noticed any problems at school having to do with Naline's race?" Sage asked.

Cimmie sat next to her on a thick protruding root. "Oh, nothing that she didn't take care of herself. One of the boys in her class was being contrary, saying things like 'you're not a real Indian' and 'Indians live on reservations,' things that basically denied her birthright. I'm sure that he didn't know that that's what he was doing."

"So what did Naline do about it?"

"She wrestled him to the ground." Cimmie shook her head. "Some move Jeff taught her. I don't know that he meant for her to use it like that, but anyway, I guess it made a believer out of him."

"Has he left her alone?" Deanne asked.

"He picked her first when they chose teams for kickball."

A smile from Deanne.

"Sometimes they manage just fine without the adults getting involved."

Sage's eyes were on the girls, who were emerged in some imaginary game. "How do you know when to leave it alone and when to step in?"

"Are you still worried about the library incident?" Cimmie asked.

Deanne replied, "I think we both are to a certain extent."

"I met with Cayley's teacher," Sage began, "and the media

teacher, and I'm not convinced that I wasn't simply being placated. For all my diplomacy, I think I got the 'recommended response' straight out of the conflict resolution chapter of the Teacher's Handbook."

"It didn't sound like they were taking it seriously," Deanne added. "They explained it away by saying that Cayley misunderstood what was being taught, and we got the impression that they think we are making too much of it. And, maybe we are. Cayley did handle it—maybe her method needs a little tweaking, but she seems capable of holding her own."

"The timing surprised me," Sage said. "I wasn't ready for a full-blown confrontation at elementary school level."

Cimmie nodded. "Me, either. I wasn't expecting anything until . . . I don't know, maybe their teens. It sounds like the girls were more ready than we were. It was never an issue with me growing up. You didn't have any problems either, did you?"

"Between threats at home and refusing to hide my sexuality, I never noticed if anyone was having a problem with my race."

"Do you think it had anything to do with us going through private school?"

"Maybe. I remember some coverage of the First Nation in the curriculum, but we had a first-rate education from NaNan, so I didn't think much about whether or not it was adequate then. But I'm concerned about it now. I know that our girls are getting what they need from us. They'll know their heritage and its rightful place in history. But what are the other students getting from the school curriculum?"

Cimmie's voice was light with new awareness. "I never gave it a thought either. Should we be surprised at being so short-sighted?"

"We're all first-time parents here," Deanne said. "What should surprise us is if we somehow did it all right—no text, no tutorial, just guessing right the first time. How lucky would that be? We shouldn't beat ourselves up. We need to take what we know now and apply it. Which brings us right back to how—and when. I think it is our responsibility to be sure that the curriculum is teaching historical truth, and that the teachers are fostering acceptance and understanding. It doesn't matter if there are a hundred Cayleys enrolled, or one, or none. It's history and it needs to be taught."

"At whose expense?" Sage asked. "You offered your book to the principal at the beginning of the year as a teaching resource, and it still hasn't been approved by the school board. It's well researched, well documented, there's no explanation other than lack of interest. When do you take your child out of a potential war zone and find a school that already recognizes the importance of inclusive education?"

"Are you talking about a private school?" Cimmie asked.

"If need be."

"Become the elitist that you claimed our mother was?"

Deanne raised her palms. "Throw up the white flag?"

"No, just fight the fight somewhere else, so that our child isn't on the battleground."

"I want to protect her, too, Sage. I'm certainly not advocating throwing her out there and watching her try to dodge the bullets. I'm convinced that there are benefits to being part of the educational process, part of the struggle, that Cayley wouldn't get in a more sheltered environment."

"Her argument for public verses private education," Sage explained. "I'm not convinced, especially now."

"I don't know," Cimmie began, "I'm leaning toward Deanne on this one. It's much like the gay struggle, don't you think? Look at the impact that Ellen DeGeneres has had. Millions of people laugh and dance with her every day. Do you think she would have had the same effect if she had thrown up the white flag and entertained only lesbian audiences?"

"You think private school would be preaching to the choir?"

"Wouldn't it be? With the personal focus off of Cayley, would you be as passionate in trying to change the public school curriculum?"

The dynamics were perfectly opposed. Sage, the flak-jacket that she had donned so early in life cinched tightly around her, and Cimmie expertly navigating beneath it. Deanne watched and listened. Venturing past that protection was a tricky maneuver, and no one did it better than Cim.

"I'm thinking," Cimmie continued, "that the people of the First Nation need to be as visible and passionate as gays and lesbians."

Sage held Cimmie's gaze for a few extra seconds. "That's an adult battle, that's my battle. Six and seven-year-olds have no business on the battlefield."

Chapter Twenty-Three

Saturday had been a monster of a day. Paced from sunrise to sunset with wonder and discovery, it was the highlight of the week. Throughout the day, Sage marveled at the girls' stamina. Six- and seven-year-olds, she decided, had way too much energy.

They were up this morning before anyone else. Whispers and scampering feet disappeared down the hall to some secret spot. Innocent sounds from these girls, this time, this day. Sage opened her eyes for confirmation. Yes, she was safely beyond it, beyond her own fearful whispers, the quiet flight, seeking safety. Beyond it and safe.

Not these girls, not like she and Cimmie. No acid-roiled stomachs for these girls, no fright-filled nights. No, never for their girls. Secret places should only save secrets, not lives. Their secret places muffle whispers and giggles, not tears, not cries held so tightly that their throats ache for relief.

Sage snugged her arms around Deanne and breathed in the smell of here and now. This is her life now, her home, her family. And she's not protecting them alone. She nuzzled the place just above Deanne's ear. Confirmed.

Deanne stirred awake. "Mmm, how long have you been awake?"

"Since the girls thought they were sneaking down the hall."

Deanne looked at the clock, then turned to face Sage. "They either have way too much energy, or we're getting old."

Sage smiled and kissed her. "They're taking advantage of every minute they have together. They need to be with each other—thank God for healthier reasons than why Cim and I needed each other."

"If Cim doesn't find a way to move here pretty soon, we'll have enough frequent flyer miles to shuttle them free for the next five years."

"This is hard for me." Sage threw off the bed sheet and got up. "If it had been up to me, they would have been living here free in one of the apartments until jobs opened up for them." She began pulling clothes from her drawers—quick motions as she spoke. "The girls should grow up together. Maybe we should move there. I could let Wendy manage the business, fly back and forth. It would be better than this." Impulse. Irrational. She finally looked up to meet Deanne's eyes.

"I don't think I should be that far away," Deanne replied as she fluffed the pillows. "Dad's health is so iffy, and I worry about Mom."

Sage dropped her hands to her sides and moved slowly to Deanne's side of the bed. "You shouldn't have to tell me that. Just ignore me when I get like this."

"How's that going to help? I want to know what you're thinking, what you're worrying about. For too much of your life, you had to keep it inside. I don't want you to feel like you ever have to do that again. Whatever it is, we can deal with it together."

"I thought about that this morning." Sage kept her eyes on Deanne's and held both her hands. "Whenever I sense any kind of threat, my first instinct is that it's up to me to do something about it. I don't naturally look for help—or expect it."

"I know that about you, honey. But, reminding yourself every now and then," she said and smiled gently, "is a really good idea."

"It makes me feel very good to know that you and Cimmie have my back, too." Sage rose and pulled Deanne into an embrace.

"And we all have those girls' backs," she said, tightening her arms around Sage's waist. "They'll never face anything like you did alone. Don't ever worry about that. Okay?" She tipped her head to search Sage's eyes. "Whether they are two miles apart or two thousand miles. And they know that, they're growing up knowing that."

"And they have each other."

Deanne nodded. "We'll figure the rest of it out, it's just going to take a little time."

"But, meantime," Sage sucked in a deep breath and picked up her clothes from the bed, "they're growing up—fast."

"We'll talk with Cim over breakfast and see what she's thinking."

CR CB CR

"You got both girls packed?" Sage asked.

Cimmie wheeled two small luggage bags into the kitchen. "It was just as easy to do them together. They're so excited. They want to know everything that we're going to do next week."

"Will you have time to take them to see Ben and Sarah?"

"It's on the schedule, along with Grandma Lena, and Jeff's mom, and a play, and shopping. It's going to be a busy week. Vacation is wearing me out faster than work."

"Speaking of which," Sage said, "what do you think about the position Connie said is going to be opening at her branch?"

"The girls already ate," Deanne said, entering the dinning room and placing breakfast on the table. "They went down to the lake one last time before they leave . . . what did I interrupt?"

"I was about to tell Sage that I haven't discussed the job possibility with Jeff yet. I want to be able to sit down and discuss it with him face to face."

"I wouldn't expect you to do anything else," Sage replied. "But, I want to know *your* thoughts on it. You'd have the apartment here for as long as you want it."

Cimmie took a bite of poached egg and wiped her mouth with the napkin. "The girls would go absolutely ape-shit."

Sage waited. It was a slam-dunk decision. The solution had always been about timing and opportunity. And like any good businesswoman knows, when you see it in time, you take it.

Otherwise, it's gone. Families, though, aren't businesses, and the extraneous attachments to family decisions added time and demanded patience. And patience was not one of Sage's best attributes. She caught Deanne watching her. *I know,* she wanted to say, *I won't push her.*

"You'd still be going back once a month to see Ben and work on getting funds for the school, wouldn't you?"

Sage nodded.

"The girls could probably go with you," Cimmie continued. "They could visit their grandmothers and friends."

Another nod, and a sip of coffee. Somehow it helped extend her patience.

"Maybe Jeff and I could, too, but not every month."

Sage broke her silence, offering what she intended as subtle help. "Do you think Lena would consider moving here?" Cimmie seemed surprised. "She would if *you* brought it up."

"I have. She doesn't see any reason to move. Do you believe her when she said that John's never tried to contact her from prison?"

"I don't know, sometimes I do, sometimes I doubt her," Cimmie replied. "She knows he couldn't have been a worse father than he was. She divorced him, though, walked away from the house, the money. How much more final could it be?"

"You *know* how much more final it could be . . . I know," she offered, lifting her hand, "that worry is gone. It's just that we have a chance to finally make this family whole, to give our girls the family we didn't have. " Don't push. Explain. Tell her your needs, not your fears. "I don't just want the girls to have what we didn't have, I want us to have that, too."

There it was. How many more conversations it had taken for her to open up to me like that. Yet, for Cimmie, Sage rips open the flak jacket and flashes her the guarded place. That sensitive place, innervated by tightly woven fears, formed so early, guarded for so long. Deanne understood the nature of it, the reason for it being, but not like Cimmie understood it.

117

Cimmie nodded, her eyes locked with her sister's. "You're afraid that Jeff doesn't get that."

Silence.

Deanne picked up the dishes and put them in the sink. "I'll go get the girls."

"Thanks, Deanne," Cimmie said. She watched her leave the room before meeting Sage's eyes again. "I know that worries you. It's hard to wait, hard to trust. But, this is the man who knowingly married into this unconventional family, the same man who fathered Naline with you, and who loves her and raises her as if she was his and mine alone."

"But will he really leave his own family and his friends? Is it right for me to expect that? Maybe it is pride that has kept him from accepting a house from me, or maybe it's actually something more."

"Give me a little more time, okay? I'm pretty sure I know that answer, but he needs to be the one to tell you what that is."

"And Lena? She's a big part of this family finally healing and feeling whole."

"Let's take one step at a time, Sage." Movement from outside the window caught Cimmie's attention. The girls were scurrying up the hill. She brought her eyes back to Sage's. "Tell Connie to send me the information on the job opening."

ʗʘ ʘʗ ʗʘ

The weekend clean-up was done. Dishes washed, laundry folded, house swept and dusted, and preps made for the upcoming week. It was only then that the change was apparent. The sounds were different. Gone were the high tones of little girls' voices and their steady stream of questions. No chairs scooting across the tile, or squeals from the other room. It was calm and quiet, and predictable.

Well, maybe not totally predictable. Deanne rested folded arms on the railing of the deck off the kitchen, and watched the sun bow behind the tall pines and leave their silhouettes outlining the shoreline. The music playing in the background turned noticeably more intimate as Sage's arm encircled Deanne's waist.

"Still think it's a bad idea to hire a housekeeper?"

"I do wonder," Deanne replied, "how two small girls and three adults can leave this looking like the aftermath of Mardi Gras when everyone picked up after themselves."

"If you let me hire someone," Sage said softly against Deanne's head, "we could spend the cleaning time doing something much more enjoyable."

A soft evening breeze lifted summer scents from the lake. Deanne breathed them in. They carried instant thoughts of summer youth and late-night mischief. "Like," she asked, turning into Sage's arms, "skinny-dipping in the lake?"

"Or, dancing on the deck," Sage teased Deanne's lips with light, tender touches of her own, "and making love under the stars?"

Deanne brushed her lips over Sage's, let the tip of her tongue outline the shape of her mouth, and whispered, "Or all of the above."

The mood was set, the opportunity perfect. The song in the background declared, "You take my breath away."

Deanne asked in a whisper, "Do I still?"

Sage kissed her, longer, more intently. Then, pulling her lips away only enough to whisper, "You do."

"In my sweaty T-shirt," Deanne returned, lifting her eyes, "and raggy shorts?"

"In anything, and nothing. How serious are you about skinny-dipping?"

Slipping from their embrace, Deanne grabbed the hem of her shirt. But, before she could strip it off, Sage's cell rang.

Instinctively, Sage grabbed it.

"Cimmie?" Deanne asked.

Sage dropped her head back and her arm to her side. "No," she groaned, "Sharon."

Deanne shook her head. "Well, we have all week. Go ahead and answer it. I'll be in the shower," she said as Sage answered the call, "but not for *that* long."

"Hey, Sharon." Sage leaned to kiss Deanne, then settled on a deck chair for the anticipated ramble.

"Hope I didn't call at a bad time."

"No, it's fine. Cim and the girls left earlier today. Dee and I have a week to ourselves."

"Yeah, I didn't want to bother you last night, but I have a little bit of information, and an idea that I want to pick your brain about."

Sage leaned forward in her chair. Sharon wasn't drunk. "Pick away," she replied.

"Jenny and I have been talking, kinda self-therapy stuff. Talking about what made Donna and Evonne such special people, you know beyond being good parents and friends. We realized that a big part of who they were was something a lot of people took for granted. They were there for anyone who needed them."

In a nutshell.

"Helping start the community center was so important to them because they saw how an organization could help so many more people than they could alone. A place for our community to help each other. A safe place."

"They'd be amazed to see it now. With increased tolerance comes a lot more money."

"I hope somehow they know what their vision became. There were a lot of people looking forward while I was too busy looking back."

"So," Sage interjected, "what is it you need to pick my brain about?"

"Would you sit down with Jenny and me—and I want to get Connie to help, too—and show us what we need to do to get the funding and set up a scholarship program? We want to be able to give an annual college scholarship for a gay or lesbian teen in Donna and Evonne's names."

"Well, that's where it's needed, all right. I can't imagine that the guidance counselors are rounding up gay teens and offering them a list of grants and scholarships to choose from."

"Yeah, a lot of them can't count on help from their family. I wasn't disowned or anything like that, but there was no way my mother could have helped me go to school. I wonder what I would have done if I could have finished college . . . Anyway, what do you think of our idea?"

"It's a great idea. Let me know when and where Connie can join us. You know, it's going to take some old-fashioned persistence. It can be frustrating, and it can take a lot longer than you think."

"Oh, hell, any other way and I wouldn't know how to act. Which brings me to the information—finally—just a little, but I'll take anything at this point. Someone inside the governor's office leaked that she'll make the decision this week."

"Any indication which way she's leaning?"

"No, but she's a lame duck. She has nothing to lose either way."

"Unless she has plans to further her political career, and she should."

"I'm thinkin' that with the pile of fat-cat shit she inherited when she took office, and the shovels she had to choose to clear a path, this decision won't even get noticed a few months from now."

"You're probably right." *And totally sober. Kasey said it, something had changed.*

"Oh, and I don't know if you've heard this, either. It'll probably be on the news tomorrow. Sarah Palin was just visiting the Kickapoo reservation in Texas—maybe because it's located in Maverick County—that, of course, only makes Palin-sense. Anyway, the spokesman for the tribe kept referring to her as Walking Eagle. So, the reporter asked him how they came up with that name for her. His answer was that no eagle full of that much shit could ever fly." Then the laugh, that raspy, contagious sound of irreverence.

Sharon had taken her, hook, line, and sinker, right to the punch line. Sage had to smile. "I need to be more careful about what I wish for."

The laughter trailed off. "What?"

"When are you coming back to card night, so that we'll have enough to actually play?"

"See, I knew you missed my jokes."

"I miss kicking your butt."

"Yeah, we'll see. I have to find a card partner. I think I'm single again."

"You think?"

"Kim's not answering my phone calls or texts."

"What happened?"

"Well, I guess I'm supposed to know that. But, besides being an asshole at times, I really don't. I'm supposed to own up to something, but if I don't know what it is, there's no sense in apologizing."

"I'm sorry, Sharon."

"Yeah, I am, too. I think."

"I'm not even coming up with any words of wisdom here that might help."

"Chances are, if it was something that would work for you, it wouldn't work for me . . . I'm okay. We're getting our butts kicked at work, I'm trying to finally finish my own house, and I have Abby to keep me company. I'd just end up pissin' off a girlfriend anyway. It's kinda nice not having to worry about it."

"So, do a card night," Sage said and smiled to herself, "and piss your friends off."

Chapter Twenty-Four

"This house is a three-bedroom, two-bath, Craftsman-style bungalow," Sharon began. "It has a finished basement, perfect for entertaining, which the owner used to do a lot of. The main floor has been recently renovated. There are refinished hardwood floors throughout, and a beautifully maintained fireplace flanked by oak and glass built-ins here in the living room. Now the kitchen," she said, motioning toward the open doorway, "was just finished yesterday and shows the owner's commitment to the original character of the house."

Abby followed Sharon into the kitchen and headed for her water bowl.

"As you can see," Sharon continued, "your bowls now rest on porcelain tile and the cabinets have all been refaced in warm hickory."

Abby had finished drinking and now sat watching Sharon, her head tilted as though she understood.

"And, the countertop, well, you're too short," she said, picking Abby up. "Quite impressive, don't you think? The rich brown brings out the darker markings in the hickory. That's according to Kasey, and I have to say I agree with her. You know, the owner got a killer deal on this granite. A broken slab with just enough real estate left for this job. Impressive, right?"

The response was a few fast licks to Sharon's ear.

"So, what do you think, Miss? Is this house to your liking? The rent is cheap. The owner accepts vigorous tail wags and wet kisses in lieu of actual dollars."

More kisses.

"Then, you'll take it. Perfect. And, with those kisses you are well on your way to a month's rent." She nuzzled a kiss to the little dog's neck. "Hey, I've got an idea. Since this is no longer an embarrassing hodge-podge of half-finished projects, let's you and I host a card night."

She placed Abby on the floor, and added, "Okay, let's try out that new handheld shower thing. I didn't want to mention it while you had that damn cast on, but you could really use a bath."

Sharon gathered the bath necessities and Abby followed along, totally unaware that "bath" was a four-letter word. She was granted a temporary reprieve, though, when the doorbell rang.

After ten by the bathroom clock. "Late-night visits or phone calls, Abbs—usually not good."

There was a strong temptation to ignore it—the comfortable way out, for now. What you don't know . . . But, not logical. Ignoring the late night calls in her past would not have changed their messages, and disassociation wasn't possible. So . . .

She opened the door and it felt as though her heart froze immediately in her chest. She couldn't breathe, couldn't suck in air, and couldn't pull her eyes from Laura's. Eyes she once knew so well, now holding things that she was afraid to know. She couldn't speak.

But Laura could. "I can't help it. I know I shouldn't be here," she said, her eyes moist with tears.

Sharon wanted to grab her and pull her tight, to tell her that she wanted her here, not to cry, that everything was all right. She wanted to in the worst way. She wanted to kiss her again, full and deep, until neither of them could breathe. Feel the softness of her, the heat of her passion, the love she had missed so much. But Sharon couldn't move. Her feet remained cemented in place, her arms hung heavily at her sides. Even her eyes, locked in an unbelieving stare, could do nothing but tear.

The only one capable of movement was Abby. She wiggled

excitedly around Sharon's legs, then immediately greeted Laura by stretching her front paws up to rest against Laura's knee.

It was as if a tether had snapped. Sharon lunged forward, picked up Abby, and the words began tumbling out. "This is Abby, my best girl. She's part of old Hank's litter, his dog's, I mean, and she took a likin' to me and—well, anyway—come in and shut the door." Laura complied and Sharon continued. "She came over all the time and I never got his fence repaired and then Danny down the street hit her and we rushed her to the hospital." Barely a breath. "I stayed with her. I couldn't leave her. It was awful, but I couldn't leave. *Now* look at her. She's getting so strong, just a tiny limp—"

"She's adorable."

"I'm rambling." Losing control. Heart beating like a jack-hammer.

"No." Laura stepped closer. "No. I want to know . . . but, I don't want to intrude in your life. I would never have stopped if the car had still been out front. But, I had to come. I had to know."

Stop looking at her eyes. Breathe, dammit, breathe. "What do you need to know?" Sharon finally forced her eyes away and focused on Abby.

"That you're okay."

"Good." Sharon nodded her head, kept her eyes down. "I'm good."

Laura took another step forward. "I know I have no right to be here. If you want me to leave, I'll understand."

She could barely hear her own words over the thudding in her chest. "If that is why you're here, to be sure that I'm okay, then you should leave." Never had she imagined saying those words. Drunk or sober, depressed or not. Never. Were they even her words? She had hoped for this day, waited for this day, and now Laura was turning to leave, and she was sure that this time she would not survive it.

But the door closed, and her heart did not stop beating. Her breathing, too, caught in impasse at the suddenness, resumed its rhythm. She was still alive, physically—standing, staring, wondering why, hoping that the whole thing was just some cruel, sadistic daydream.

Exactly when she had placed Abby on the floor, she couldn't say. Abby had made her way up the carpeted ramp to the couch, and picked her ears up as Sharon turned.

The quivering in her legs as Sharon crossed the room surprised her. She bounced her fists against the hard, thick muscles of her thighs trying to make it stop. "What have I done, Abby?" She eased down onto the couch and welcomed Abby on her lap. She whispered it this time. "What have I done?"

There she sat, the quivering now in her stomach, unable to move, an unshakable impulse pummeling her chest. *Get up. Go after her. Do it. Tell her you want her in your life. Do it before it's too late. Get up!*

But she couldn't. Whatever it was that kept her there—self-preservation, fear of being right—whatever it was, it had her strapped down and paralyzed. And she wondered, after years of wishing her back, how anything or anyone could strap her down like that.

She dropped her head back and rested it against the couch. "Of all the times," she said softly, "that I've been wrong, why this time do I have to be right?"

Sharon squeezed her eyes shut. A wet stream made its way down her jaw line. She didn't wipe it or try to stop it; she just let it go.

ରେ ଓଷ ରେ

It was over. Finally.

Sharon lay on the bed, her face pressed against a sleeping Abby, the last of her tears wetting the soft curls. A night of tears, of mourning, finally. The loss she could never touch, never own. It was done now. She'd freed herself, cut the tie herself, and now all she could do was hope that the doctor was right.

This time, no alcohol to dull the pain, nothing but tears to rinse away the toxicity of the hope she had held. This time she'd do it right. She'd face the loss, let it be ugly and painful, and she'd get through it.

Abby stirred beside her, stretched the full length of her tiny frame and pushed tighter against Sharon's chest. Carefully Sharon moved her arm to rest gently around Abby. She closed her eyes and listened to the deep, even breathing, and felt the rise and fall against her chest. *A blessing she hadn't counted on, but counted now. One of many. It was time to count them, the many blessings. Name them, one by one by one.*

Chapter Twenty-Five

Sharon sat in the truck, Abby on her lap, staring at the river from the edge of the parking lot. The water flowed smoothly there around the narrow bend just before it broke into a rough tumble over dark boulders half-buried in the river's bed. A little bit of a tricky launch to get a canoe or kayak far enough out into the middle and get a better angle between the rocks before taking the rapids. A slightly easier task to maneuver a truck inner tube, as long as you don't mind getting wet.

"Tubin', Abbs. That's what we did on our first date."

Abby looked up at her and cocked her head.

"Right here. I made her wear old tennis shoes and stay up high on the tube until we got clear of the rocks. Laura'd never been tubin' before. I was afraid that she was going to be a real wuss."

Sharon reached across the seat and picked up a small yellow box. "Come on, Abbs, let's go for a walk."

The word was a favorite, near the top of Abby's fast-growing vocabulary. She pushed her front paws repeatedly against the door.

"Okay, okay. Let's get your leash on here." Sharon opened the door and placed Abby on the ground. "There." She gave Abby a long lead and followed her to the water's edge.

"Sometimes it seems like yesterday," she said aloud. "Other times . . ." She surveyed the stretch of water as the ruffles smoothed once more into an easy flow down past the low rapids. It hadn't changed, even though it had been years since she had last walked the shoreline. Native plants hugged the bank, creeping between large boulders, defining the river's boundary and directing its course. The boundary maintained the parkland for a mile or so before private yards descended to claim a share of the north bank.

They wandered along the south bank, Abby investigating low-flying dragonflies and floating twigs as they bumped against the rocks, and Sharon revisiting the beginning of a love affair.

The bridge, made of iron and wood, had been strategically built at a point just before the river widened, to serve foot traffic and one car at a time. Halfway across, Sharon stopped, leaned her forearms on the railing and watched a female mallard ride the slower-moving flow downriver.

The weather had been much like today's, clear and bright, the temperature cooling as the air whisked across the surface of the water. She could almost feel the motion of the water again, carrying the giant truck tube down the river. Her hand was linked with Laura's, keeping them close as the current pulled them. They laid their heads back against the warmth of the tube, let their feet dangle motionless in the water. It was all about getting to know a little about each other, about wondering if "I" could become "we," and letting fate, like the current of the river, take them where it would.

Laura was Tom Sawyer, making her way down the Mississippi—an adventure complete with a peek at life along the river. There were sloping manicured yards and wild ones, weathered wood docks, and people enjoying their summer weekend, cooking and playing and sunbathing nude on the big rocks. There were waves and greetings, and not a more perfect day that Sharon could remember. The sky had been its purest blue, the river their perfect host. How easy it had been to laugh and talk, and fall in love.

Sharon looked down at the little yellow box. "I guess it's time, Abbs," she said, touching her fingertips over the top of the box.

Abby looked up from her spot at the base of the bridge's railing. She had been waiting patiently, somehow sensing the somber mood of this long pause in their walk.

"No tears, though, little girl. I promise. It's just time to say goodbye, that's all." She opened the box. Lifted it to see if the fragrance was still detectable, then slowly emptied the contents over the rail. She watched the once bright red petals, now dried and muted, as they fell gently to the water's surface. She continued to watch until the river carried them out of sight.

"It's symbolic, Abbs, like Dr. Talbot said. The first rose from Laura's rosebush. So, it's gone now, you know, just like the love we once had together. I made it visual, just like she said to." Her eyes teared despite her promise, and Sharon quickly closed the box and wiped her eyes with the sleeve of her T-shirt.

"Okay, she said, picking Abby up and kissing her firmly on the head, "we did it . . . it's supposed to start getting better now." Abby wiggled anxiously. "Yeah, you've been very patient. I'll bet we can find something to do that will make us both feel better. Let's give it a try. Okay?"

Chapter Twenty-Six

It took three days to muster the courage. The number to Connie's office glared at her from the cell phone. Laura took a deep breath and hit the call button.

"If you know the extension of the person you are calling, enter it now. If not, say the last name of the person now."

"Bradford." Another concentrated breath.

Still time to change her mind.

"This is Connie Bradford. How can I help you?"

Last chance to back out. A rush of nervous energy. Voice slightly unsure, "Connie, this is Laura Jamison." *She won't hang up, not Connie.*

Her tone rested easily in that space between professional and personal. "Hi, Laura. How have you been?"

Unlike most, Laura knew Connie really expected an honest answer. "I've been better," she replied, "and I've been worse. But I called because I wondered if you would meet me for lunch one day."

"Actually, the rest of the week I'm tied up at lunch. I'll be eating here and working through . . . will today work?"

"Yes," Laura replied quickly, "today is perfect."

"There's a little restaurant in the strip mall on the same side of the street about a mile west of me, Corner Kitchen. Homemade desserts and the absolute best coffee on the planet. Is that too far for lunch, at about 12:15?"

"It's fine. I'm salaried, so I can make up the time."

"Then I'll see you in a couple of hours."

The aroma was a decadent mix of fresh ground coffee beans, and vanilla and chocolate; the feeling it offered was a pampered sense of well-being. Comfort scents, holding memories of mother's early morning off-to-work hugs, and grandma's special baking days. Warm and sweet, the feeling wrapped her with familiarity that leaned her comfortably forward and rested her gaze easily on her one-time friend.

Their cordial greeting and surprisingly warm hug behind them, Laura began right away with the inevitable question. "How is everyone?"

Connie spoke, as she always had, as much with her eyes as she did with words. There was a hesitation as her focus seemed to soften, to envelop the concern in Laura's eyes. "Right now," she said, "everyone is fine."

"I wouldn't ask if I really didn't care. I hope you know that about me."

Connie offered a gentle smile. "I do. I've been on your end of the discussion before, so I know how hard this is for you."

"That's why I called you. You've always made me feel comfortable. I've missed you—your friendship . . . I've missed you all."

"You know that I can only speak for myself. I've missed you, too."

"I'm quite clear on how Kasey feels." *And sure that everyone else is clear on that as well.* "And it's good to know that not everyone feels the same as she does."

Before it could become uncomfortable, Connie cut seconds of silence short. "So, let's see, how do I summarize?" She thought a moment while a waitress delivered salads and homemade soup, and then hustled on to another table. "Some times it seems like a lifetime ago . . . economically it's been tight, but, I'm still working and Kasey and Sharon are doing most of the physical work again to keep the company afloat. Deanne is working on her fourth book, and Sage's company is set up to do well regardless of the economy. Their little girl is almost seven now."

A beam of a smile instantly replaced careful reservation. "Sage is a mom," Laura said, more as a statement than a question.

"Well, Deanne is mom, and Cayley speaks Seneca, so she calls Sage nu' ye—Seneca for mother."

"Who would've thought?"

"Deanne, for one. She kept saying how good Sage is with kids. But I would guess there are more than a few women in Sage's past who'd be dropping their jaws."

"It makes me think of the baby shower we did for Cimmie. I haven't laughed that hard since. Just the thought—" a laugh began, creasing into crow's feet.

A burst of air sputtered from between Connie's lips. "Sage wearing that belly—oh, my God, that was funny."

Laura nodded, eyes squeezed shut in a futile attempt at control. "And Ali," she squeaked out, tears leaking from the corners of her eyes, "throwing that baby doll—"

"The biggest femme in the group, and all she could say was 'fuck it' and throw that doll."

They were both laughing now—unexpectedly, letting it burst free and unabashedly connect memory after memory. They laughed and reminisced while their soup cooled and their salads sat untouched. For a while they could be old friends, revisiting a time they both wished they had back.

"That feels so good," Laura said, "to laugh like that again. I have missed it so much."

"Even when it was at Sharon's expense?"

"Oh, listen, a big part of our relationship involved her bouncing things off me, and me taming them into something at least close to socially acceptable, and then watching her blow holes in the parameters. My personal challenge was to get past any embarrassment so that I could laugh. Then it was fun."

"The dynamic you two had together was special."

Laura nodded. Her tone changed noticeably. "It was."

Then the question that had waited years to be asked. "What happened, Laura?"

Laura's relief was evident, the lines around her eyes softened, the hold of her shoulders eased. "I've wanted to answer that for a long time, but I didn't think anyone really wanted to know."

"It's quite a mixed bag, you have to know that. From Kasey's long-time loyalty to Sharon, to Sage's 'It's really none of my business.' But, for me, it's time to know, time to hear what Sharon's never going to say anyway."

"Thank you. I only hope that you aren't going to be sorry that you asked. It's going to sound a lot more simplistic than it is." Laura's eyes remained solidly on Connie's. "I found myself doing to Sharon what my mother did to my father. She loved him and she enabled him, and he drank himself to death. He was loved, but he never got the help that he needed. I loved Sharon too much to do that to her."

"Do you think Sharon is an alcoholic?"

"I think I believed that at one point. It was the easiest answer. Everything got so complicated. The anger and depression and the drinking. I couldn't be sure which was the root cause of the others, and she wouldn't get help. I wanted to help her—I tried. I did everything I could think of." She leaned forward, signs of anguish apparent on her face. "We'd talk it through and I'd fool myself into believing it was getting better. She hid it so well from everyone, even me for a while. She'd have card nights, and joke with everyone. She even planned that shower, but each day I could feel her slipping further away from me. Nearly every minute that she wasn't working or with you all, she was obsessing about injustice—writing, calling, e-mailing, drinking . . . I help people recover, Connie, that's what I do, help them come back from injuries and surgeries. I put my hands on them and physically help them. But, I couldn't put my hands on Sharon's pain. I couldn't help her . . . and I couldn't stay any longer and watch her self-destruct."

"Personally, I don't think anything or anyone can help them until they're ready. I was lucky, Kasey pulled herself through it. But, everyone deals with tragedy in their own way. Sharon has lost so many people in her life. There's no biological family left that I know of, so she put together a family of people she loved and trusted. And, then someone took a big part of *that* away. It was like something kept happening that she was powerless to stop."

"And, then I left, too."

"Something else that she had no power over, or at least she thought she couldn't control it . . . I won't sugarcoat it, she was a mess, worse than when you were there. But, when she realized that she was in danger of losing Kasey and the business, too, she finally agreed to get help."

"And she's doing well?"

"She still has her ups and downs, but Kasey thinks that she's been able to find a balance easier lately . . . It may sound—I don't know, maybe too Hollywood, but Sharon saved this little dog and since then she's been like a different person. It's made us realize something. Sharon not only needs to be needed, she needs to know that she's made a difference. I never would have thought that something so little could have such a huge impact. It's hard to tell who saved who."

Laura hesitated before saying, "I know." Another hesitation. "I saw her, Connie. I went to her house. I know I shouldn't have. You don't have to tell me that. I know. It was selfish. It was—"

"Necessary."

Surprise registered on Laura's face. The response, even from Connie, was so unexpected. "It was. It really was." *Necessary. The word was perfect.* The one she hadn't been able to find on her own. "And I'm sure that you are the only one that understands that. Even I don't. I gave myself permission to see her, but I question my reason."

"Even after you saw her?"

"Especially after I saw her. I could see that it shook her—she clung to little Abby like a shield. Whether the message was a conscious one or not, I got it—I wasn't welcome past Abby, physically or vocally."

"You're questioning why you needed to see her?"

"I guess I am . . . It seems like we both assumed I was there to be sure that she was okay. There was no actual discussion, only her saying that if that was why I was there then I should leave, and me leaving."

"I've got a real thing about assumptions. They're too easy to rely on, and they can cause so much damage."

"I tried to be careful about that. I didn't want to assume that she'd want to see me, or that she would be single, or that she hadn't self-destructed. But, as for myself . . ."

"So, why did you need to see her?"

Her brow knitted tightly above her nose before Laura spoke. "I've never met anyone in my life with as much honest passion about anything as Sharon. She believes devoutly in what she's doing, so much so that she ignores her own vulnerability. People like that do make a difference, even if they never see it themselves."

"There's something else I've realized," Connie began. "I noticed how Sage interacts with Sharon. She never discourages her from talking about politics or causes, and she always tells her how important her efforts are. Sharon's like Kasey, used to seeing immediate fruits of her labor. When they build something, fix something, paint and stain, they control the outcome. They see it through, make it right. What Sage knows from years of being involved in political fund-raising, and organizations like HRC, is that immediate gratification is relative, even unlikely. The results that you're fighting for could be years away, or never come at all."

"Then she understands Sharon better than most."

"Maybe even better than Kasey. On the surface there couldn't be two more different people, but beyond appearances there's something that they really get about each other."

"Something I didn't even get living with her—still don't get, I guess." Laura lowered her eyes, while the sting of the realization chastised her. "Is it a fool who doesn't learn life's lessons until the damage is done?"

"A fool wouldn't care."

"You're being kind," Laura relied, "as usual."

"So, what happens from here?"

"This fool will take care of her mother and hope that you will stay in touch with her."

Connie picked up the check from beside Laura's plate and offered a smile. "I can do that."

Chapter Twenty-Seven

"Shit!" Sharon shouted. "Shit, shit, shit!"

Kasey dropped the toolbox and snapped upright in the back of the truck. "Okay, I'm afraid to ask."

Sharon had stopped halfway to the garage. She turned and threw her arms in the air. "The car," she called back. "The neighbor's car. Damn," she said, dropping her arms hard to her sides. "Why am I so slow?"

"What are you talking about?"

Sharon started back toward the back of the truck and pointed toward the front of the house. "That's the neighbor's car parked out there, Kase. That's the same one that was parked out in front of my house when Kim came by. It took me all damn day to put two and two together after he asked me this morning if he could park it out there again."

Kasey offered a questioning shrug.

"*That's* what Kim saw, the neighbor's damn car, not the car of some secret lover. She thought I was seeing someone else and lying to her about it. That's why she's so pissed."

"So, why didn't she just ask you whose car it was?"

"And spare me all this drama? What fun would that have been?"

"Kim didn't look like she was having all that much fun."

"Then she wasted a great opportunity."

"For the record," Kasey said, dropping down to sit on the tailgate, "I don't find anything funny about torturing you."

"So, that smile on your face is sympathy."

"Hey, you've got another shot here, what's not to like about that? Unless you don't want it."

"I've been trying to do what you told me, what Dr. Talbot told me, to let go of stuff. I've been trying to concentrate on something positive. But, I just get the lid down on something, everything nice and contained, and then something blows the lid up and stuff's flyin' all over the place, and everything gets so confusing."

For a moment Kasey watched her—Sharon, the girl who had no qualms going chin to chin with the bullies on the playground, thrown off-balance by a misunderstanding. The dots weren't lining up.

"Why don't you take some time today to talk to her." Kasey jumped down from the tailgate. "Let's get the rest of the stuff into the truck, and after you help me unload at the house, go ahead and go talk to her. I'll get everything set up while you're gone."

CR CS CR

She had to admit it, she really loved how this place smelled—freshly baked breads and ground coffee beans, more varieties of both than Sharon had known existed. *She gave Kim a hard time about it only because everything in the place was organic. Well, there was the fact that she was managing the store now—what's so great about organic, how do you know that it really is organic, does it really cost three times more to produce it? Managers should know these things, or at least provide a little entertainment trying to satisfy a curious customer.*

No hard time today, though, not about the food anyway. Just a face to face that Kim had refused to allow. It may be only a few minutes, but enough for an explanation was all she was asking for. *Just an explanation. She had to try.*

Sharon stepped to the counter, wedged between chest-high glass cases filled with breads and cheeses, and asked a new hire for the manager.

Kim emerged from the office as quickly as a manager should. Her face said *I expected this,* her words, "Bren, if you need me for anything, I'll be outside."

'Outside' was an extension of the eat-in corner of the store. And since it was well past the lunch rush, it offered them a choice of tables. They settled at one behind the cement planter before either of them spoke.

Kim spoke first. "It took you longer than I thought." She relaxed against the back of the plastic chair, perfect nonchalance.

"To show up here, or finally figure out what you thought I did?"

"What was there to figure out?"

"That you thought I was cheating, and then lying about it— you saw a car parked out front. I didn't make the connection until the neighbor asked me this morning if he could park it out there again. My neighbor's second car. He had a coming-home party for his son. He set up tables in the garage and parked the car in front of my house for a couple of days. An old beige Honda, right?"

Kim leaned forward, resting her forearms on the table. Management mode in full view. "So in those three weeks that you didn't have time for me, you were just working and taking care of Abby. No other reason. No one else."

"Pretty much. Look, I haven't lied to you. I needed to deal with something on my own, that's all."

"Does *something* have a name?"

Sure. Go right to the deal-breaker. No sense messin' around in probabilities. Run right to the dead end and claim it.

"Laura's here, in town." *Wasted breath.* Kim had already pushed back into her chair, set the distance. "Let me explain, please. She did come to the house."

"Why are you here, Sharon?"

"Because I told her to leave. I needed to do it, on my own. I even did the whole symbolic saying goodbye thing and threw something of hers away."

Silent, but not totally shut down yet.

Sharon continued. "Look, I'm far from perfect, and I'll be the first one admitting it. But, I don't lie and I don't cheat. You can accuse me of being obsessive, or rude, or any number of other shortcomings I have, but don't accuse me of something I haven't done."

The hard line of Kim's brow softened. Quick to assume, just as quick to own the mistake. "I'm sorry, Sharon . . . I jumped right to the worst scenario. I'm really sorry. You didn't deserve that. It came out of my own shortcomings."

"You come by that one honestly. I can't say I wouldn't be just as suspicious if my ex was as good a liar as yours. But then, if I'd found out that my lover had been sleeping with my best friend for five months, I'd be doing my dating in the Huron Valley Correctional yard."

The laugh of diversionary magic. "So, which one would you have strangled?"

"First? Oh, that would be the one close enough to get both hands on. The problem is, one of them would have gotten away."

"Equally at fault?"

"That's not even a legitimate question. But, I have one. How *did* you walk away without strangling one of them?"

A shrug and a smile. "Somewhere in my cache of instincts must be one that let me know that all I would have gotten out of that was a long visit to that fertile HVC dating ground."

"You have great self-preservation skills," Sharon offered with a nod. "My shrink's got me identifying these kinds of skills. She thinks it will help me bolster my own. I think she has more faith in that working than I do."

"I must have gotten some of those skills from my mother. Actually, I'm more like her than I like to admit. She'd walk away and work through the hurt. I do that, too, and consider that the lesson learned will make life better for me down the road. But, right alongside that is an undeniable attraction to the kind of personality that would kick ass and ask questions later. My mother has been dealing with the yin and yang that is my father from Day One. She loves his nonconformity, his desire to right the wrongs, but all along she's tried to tame the passion that he needs to do that, because it sucks the life out of what is fun and easy about him . . . You asked me once what I see in you, why I would want to be with you . . . Well, there you have it—the yin and yang that, just like my mother, I hate to love."

"You never told me this."

"I never took the time to figure it out. It was easy not to, until that early release thing happened and you suddenly turned into my father. Even then, I tried not to put too much thought to it. We all have this notion, don't we, that who our parents are has no bearing on the 'I'm my own person, forging my own path' belief that we're so sure of. They are who they are for most of our growing up, and then without realizing it we've made this personal vow to never make the same choices that they made. Why doesn't someone warn us earlier that those tracks are set in cement?"

"Would you have believed them?"

"Of course not."

Sharon laughed at the honesty, marveled at the revelation. "Your father?" She shook her head. "So, you think those tracks you didn't know were there, led you to pick someone like your mother picked when you really wanted just the opposite. Did I get that right?"

"You did. But, hearing it said back makes it sound way too simplistic."

"Maybe because it is that simple. I'm not what you're looking for."

"Actually, you are a lot of what I'm looking for, in a friend and in a lover. Coming here today, caring about what I think, and believe—I love the person that you are. And the past couple of weeks has made me look at what we've been doing—and more importantly—where we're going, instead of floating mindlessly from day to day. I also realized that I never considered if this is what you wanted, either."

"So, we've both been floating day to day."

"But, I think, for different reasons. Me, because I'm still figuring out what I want. You, because you can't let go of what you want."

"I was with you until that last part."

"You know what I'm talking about, and you know I'm right. And if I believe what you told me today, then I have to believe you won't lie to me about this either. Unless you're still lying to yourself."

"If I'm not going to lie to you, why would I lie to myself?"

"Because maybe you want it to be different . . . but it just isn't."

"Spell it out for me."

"What you want is Laura. What you can't let go of is the possibility that you could be together again—"

"I told her—"

Kim held up her hand. "You told her to leave. I know. I believe you. I'm not saying that it's even a possibility—but possible or not, in your heart that's what you want. So, if I was ready to commit to a relationship with you, to let this become that vulnerable kind of love, where would that put you? Aren't you still here because I'm not ready for that? What we were doing together fit perfectly into your limbo world. It made us happy for as long as we needed it."

Dead end. When did twenty-eight-year olds get so smart? Or is it just this one? What the hell was I thinking at twenty-eight? How to make more money? How to get out of a dead-end job? I don't even remember. I certainly didn't recognize a dead-end relationship until it slapped me up side my head.

"I wish I could say that you're wrong. I've been pretty self-centered without even knowing it. Is that really possible? Or am I sort of unconsciously denying that too? I'm confusing *myself*."

"Hey, I'm just figuring this out myself. At least we're talking, we're trying to make sense of it instead of making it worse. We can do this without hurting each other."

"What does *that* say? That we didn't care enough about each other?"

"What's enough? Thinking that you cheated or lied, hurt. Knowing that you didn't, matters. Why does anger or hurt have to be the measuring stick for how much you care about someone? And can't you say the word 'love' without it taking on an exclusiveness that's impossible to live with?"

Sharon stared.

Kim tilted her head and waited.

"I think you were born a hippy," Sharon said.

Kim's smile was the one Sharon loved most. The wide, show-lots-of-white, spread-the-freckles smile that she knew she would miss.

"Must be in the genes. Or in the cannabis."

"It doesn't matter where it comes from. I love it. There, I said that word. So, do I go straight to hell?"

"You know what would be most painful?"

"If hell had no queers?"

Another wonderful smile. "If we couldn't still be friends no matter who we may end up in a relationship with."

"Whew. At least we might be able to control that one."

Chapter Twenty-Eight

"You know what, Abbs? There's a lot to be said about being single."
Sharon smiled at the large ears perked at attention. "And some
of it is good . . . now, I don't mean completely single, like alone. No,
nobody wants that—well, unless you're a true hermit. And, you and
me, we're just too social for that. You think I'm strange now, try
locking me away from people. Uh huh, they'd have to lock me up
all right."

Sharon propped open the screen door to the back porch, and
picked up her coffee cup and Abby's breakfast bowl. "Like this
morning," she said as Abby followed her to the porch steps. "We
can spend Sunday sitting right here, having a little breakfast,
playing a little catch, watchin' for chippies on the woodpile. And,
as long as Kasey doesn't need me, we don't have to go anywhere
if we don't want to."

Abby politely lifted her eyes, but continued to enjoy her
chicken and rice breakfast. "You know, a weekend morning like
this, Kim would have me at that music thing in the park, or
riding that borrowed bike again on those bike trails. My butt
and that bike seat, well, let's just say puberty and Kotex come
to mind. Not something that you would know—oh shit—but
you will, unless . . ."

Abby, oblivious to the ramification of such a revelation, was
pushing up the box lid to get her ball. "Okay, don't pinch your
nose." Before Sharon had the ball in her hand, Abby was already
down the steps and racing across the yard. "Yeah, that operation
is gonna have to wait," she said, tossing the ball to the back of

the yard. "You've had more than your share of down time . . . I can't think of doing that to you now."

It made her happy, watching Abby like this, begging to play, full of energy, only a hint of the trauma that almost ended her life. It made her breathe deep and easy, and smile at nothing in particular. It made her believe again—in the existence of that good place, where the elements are all in alignment and you can feel the 'rightness' of it. She would stay here forever if she could, in this space and time that defied dimension. She would let it be her place of peace, her personal joy for as long as possible. Then, she would find it again as soon as she could.

This time it lasted until the phone rang. Sharon held up the next throw and pulled the phone from her belt. "Hey, Jenny," she greeted, still smiling at the anxious little dog now standing on her hind legs at the back of the yard. "What's going on?"

"I just got a phone call this morning," Jenny replied, "from Jeremy Crawford."

The private place of 'rightness' was gone. "What did *he* want?"

"To meet with me and talk. He didn't want to talk over the phone, he wants to sit down with me. Today."

"You don't have to do that, Jenny. If you don't feel comfortable, just tell him to . . . just tell him you'd rather not."

"I think I should, meet him, I mean. But . . ."

"If it was me, you *know* what I'd tell him, but you should do what's right for you. If you really think you should, then meet him somewhere public where Brad can go with you."

"No. I want you to go with me."

Sharon stopped her five-step pacing at the bottom of the steps and sat down. Abby hurried back, pushed her front paws against Sharon's shin and turned quickly to run. One futile flat-out, ears back trip with no throw, and she was back with another push to Sharon's shin. This time, a tentative run and a look back. Nothing.

"Sharon?"

"Yeah. Dammit, Jen, you know I'll do anything for you." Abby had given up and returned to sit as patiently as she could at

Sharon's feet. "Don't you think having Brad there would have more impact—throw that medieval chest to chest thing at him?"

"Brad's always been very supportive, he'd do whatever I needed him to. But, I think you and I need to do this . . . You've known me since I was a little girl. There's no one I trust more than you to . . . honor, I guess that's the best word for it, to honor my mothers' memory. Please do this with me."

Sharon took a deep breath, tilted her head back, and marveled for just a moment at how clear and blue something can be one moment and gone the next. "Bring restraints. I can't give you any guarantees."

A laugh lifted above the apprehension. "Brad will be standing by with bail money."

ଔ ଔ ଔ

They said very little to each other as they traveled across town to a small city park. Outside, public place, surrounded with the playful sounds of children's voices and the stops and starts of residential traffic. Innocuous, emotionally diffused.

Totally not possible, diluting a toxic sea with an eyedropper. But, for Jenny's sake, she would hold her breath for as long as she could.

He stood as they approached, extended his hand to Jenny, offered eye contact to Sharon. "Thank you for coming," he began. "I didn't expect to see you both, but I'm glad you came."

Sharon looked away, picked out two little boys full of adventure and imagination, and focused on their game. *They were in that perfect place where control was theirs and the world was what they made it. She'd been there before, she and Ronnie, pirates on the High Seas. The old wooden trailer with the flat tire, stored out behind the garage, had become the baddest ship on the ocean. A torn bed sheet, an old steering wheel, ropes and paint bucket kegs and, if you balanced just right over the axle, the perfect roll of the ocean waves. Captain 'D' and first mate*

Ron 'D' staving off the raids of the Jenkins twins and the neighborhood crews. Hidden treasure moved and guarded, stolen and recaptured. Their fantasy, their perfect world.

She'd watch them, Sharon decided, decipher their world and let their adventure take her away from this deranged man and his insane mission.

The boys filled her vision, had her attention, but nothing blocked the sound of Jeremy Crawford's voice.

"I wanted to tell you personally," he was saying, "and not have you hear it on the news."

Sharon concentrated harder on the boys' adventure. *Not pirates, not cowboys. Come on, block his voice out.*

"Tell us what?" Jenny asked.

Surely she's not ready for the decision that gave him license for this guilt-effacing personal report. Must she ask?

"My father passed away early this morning."

Sharon's attention snapped back around, first to Jenny, then to Jeremy. She felt as if she'd been sucker-punched. *Why wasn't she prepared for this? All her focus on the possible release, the decision facing the governor, all that energy and anger—so little thought that it could all end so quickly.*

Jenny dropped her focus, lowered her head, said nothing.

What was there to say? Justice had been served? That you're glad he's dead?

Jeremy, too, changed his focus. Looked away toward the children on the swings.

The swing chains squeaked and excited voices challenged to push higher. Jenny's voice finally broke in. "Thank you," she said, "for telling us. It couldn't have been an easy thing to do."

Sharon felt herself nod. The words part of a natural course. "I thank you, too . . . I'm not sure how to react right now."

"That's all right," he said, his eyes returning to meet Sharon's. "I'm sort of at a loss myself. I thought I knew how I would feel when he died. I knew how it was supposed to feel, the normal grief of losing a parent. My mother passed away two years ago, so I suppose I expected to feel much the same way that I felt then. But I don't. I feel mostly relief."

"Until this minute," Jenny began, "I haven't thought about how hard it would be for you. It had to be difficult all these years to continue loving your father and at the same time hate what he had done. We didn't have that conflict. Our conflict is trying to forgive him."

"I've dealt with that, too, but it started a long time ago when I was just a kid. I blamed him for tearing our family apart, and I struggled for years looking for a way to forgive him for that."

"And did you forgive him?" Jenny asked.

"For the most part. But, it took hurting my mother before I could see who he was. I insisted that I be allowed to live with him. I was so sure that I was missing something special, and that she was keeping me from it. It didn't seem to affect my sisters the same way that it did me. I wanted that regular family that most of my friends had, mother and father and the kids living in the same house. And when I couldn't have that, I was determined not to lose my father. But, living with him wasn't at all what I expected."

"To be honest," Sharon said, "and I'm not trying to inflict any more pain for you here, but I don't care if I ever find a way to forgive him for what he did." She looked to Jenny. "I know Jenny's trying, and she's got a much better shot at forgiveness than I do."

"I'm not there yet," Jenny added. "Maybe if I knew why, it would help."

"If I could tell you that, I would," he said. "My father was an angry man. At least, that's what he turned into later in his life. His anger seemed to grow out of frustration and his inability to control what was happening to him. My mother thought that he had unrealistic expectations when he got out of the service. He could never get the job he really wanted, my mother ended up leaving him, he didn't have his kids. It all kept piling up on him. And as I got older, I saw how he turned everything into a personal attack. If the city raised the taxes, he saw it as an attempt

149

to force him out of his house. The county snowplow piling snow at the end of his drive and not at the neighbor's across the street was an attempt to trap him in his house."

"So, what kind of personal attack could have cost two women their lives?" Sharon asked.

Jeremy shook his head. "I wish I knew. I wish I had seen it coming. I was there just two days before. He was complaining about everything from spoiled fruit from the market and bank fees going up, to selling the property next door twenty-some years ago. Nothing stood out as anything to be concerned about."

"The property he sold, was that Mom's?"

He nodded. "He had to split up the acreage in the divorce. He had always wanted one of us kids to live there."

"So, he ends up with lesbians," Jenny replied, "instead of his kids and grandkids."

"And a fence," Sharon added, "just screamin', 'This is no longer yours. Stay out.' Maybe it was a combination of things. Who would have figured, though, that it would result in that kind of anger and hate?"

"Maybe if I had been listening better, or taking his spoutings seriously. Maybe I could have—"

"Yeah, maybe," Sharon said. "But he wasn't crazy and he wasn't defending himself. *He* was responsible. What good does it do for you to shoulder any of the blame? And I really want to know why you would go to so much effort to bring him home. All that did was stir up the emotions and anger all over again."

No immediate answer, only the need for one hanging between them. They waited, Jenny watching Sharon, Sharon watching Jeremy.

He leaned forward and rested on the rough wooden surface. As he spoke, his focus remained on his hands with their fingers intertwined, reminiscent of a small child's prayer. "You would think that I would know that, wouldn't you? The truth is," he lifted his head, "I never thought about why. I was being the good son, doing the right thing for his father. I wanted it to be the right thing—for my kids, for my family . . . I wanted normal. I've always wanted that. You know, the normal family, normal father—coaching my little league team, spending lazy Saturday afternoons on a riverbank, someone to go to for sound advice. I was trying to honor *that* parent. But he wasn't that parent. He tried, with varying degrees of success, but there was too much that he couldn't deal with. I clung hard to those better times all of my life. So, if there is a 'why' to my doing this, that's probably it. And now, all I can say is that I'm sorry that I've caused you so much pain."

Jenny was first to respond. "Ultimately, does it matter where he died?"

"It does," he replied. "I realize that now. I was impeding the message, watering it down with my personal issues. Without meaning to, I was saying that the hate that killed your mother had some justification. And the sad thing is that I wouldn't have realized it in time had he not died before the governor made a decision. I would have allowed the impact, however helpful, to be lost."

Sharon released a long audible sigh. "Why aren't you a pit bull? I wanted you to be a pit bull." She acknowledged his puzzled look, and played on it. "Snarling through barred teeth, long strings of drool hangin' from your jowls."

His laugh was unexpected, medicinal. "That's what you wanted me to be like? Why?"

"I've been facing down pit bulls all my life. I know how to do that."

"So, this confused mongrel has disappointed you."

"No," Jenny replied. "You've made us do what we've been expecting everyone else to do. Donna and my mother would have expected nothing less of us."

"You didn't have to talk to us today," Sharon added. "You didn't have to talk to us at all. But I'm glad you did. I'm not sure I would've had the chutzpah if I'd been in your shoes."

"I have no doubt that you would have," he said. "That's one

reason why I'm here." He rose from the table, and extended his hand, first to Jenny and then to Sharon.

This time, Sharon grasped it firmly. "Thank you," she said.

They watched as he left, hands in his pockets, head tall.

"It is easier to hate," Sharon remarked, "isn't it?"

Chapter Twenty-Nine

Such a strange feeling. It had stayed with Sharon all day Sunday. Jenny, too, had noticed it—the lack of jubilation in their voices as they made the phone calls, the brevity of their e-mails and texts. There wasn't the expected celebration of Charlie Crawford's death, only acknowledgement. A skirmish had been won, and the war goes on.

There was, though, a sense of calm—a gentle swaying of the boat as the world righted itself. It felt unusually good, and not even a Monday, hot and humid and physically demanding, was going to change that.

"Ready for demolition duty?" Troy asked, handing Sharon the long bar.

"Always. Cheap therapy, great anger management." She slipped her hammer into the metal hanger on her belt and smiled. "Knocking down this old deck last week might have saved me a shrink visit."

"Ooh, sorry," he flashed an A-list movie-star smile and pulled loose a section of rotted railing. "This bad girl had to wait until I got the upstairs painted. I guess you guys are gonna rent this one out, eh?"

"Yeah, on a six-month lease. We're keeping it listed, but it takes so long for the banks to close on sales that we have to have some income from it meantime."

"Okay, then let's get to it. Kasey's at the county building, but she'll be here with the lumber in an hour. I think we can get the structure done today."

She loved working with Troy. He was smart and strong, worked through pain and could chitchat as well as any woman without missing a swing of the hammer. A multitasking male—they do exist.

It seemed there was nothing too much to tackle amid stories of his youthful escapades, and the laughter—the much-needed, much-appreciated laughter. Today, though, stories of his precocious five-year-old son made the world seem permanently balanced.

"Yep, Jimmy John the miniature carpenter was devastated that he couldn't come to work with me today. He is convinced that we cannot get this thing down today without his help. He about broke my heart, sitting there on the boot bench by the back door, that little tool belt you got him strapped around his waist, and ready to go—damn, he makes it hard to say no."

"So, why not bring him?"

"Too dangerous today. Too much stuff flying and falling, rotten wood, rusty nails."

"Yeah, of course, exactly why I didn't bring Abby today. I never realized how hard it is to say 'no.' Sometimes being a responsible adult just plain sucks."

"It does," he said, then laughed. "I tried to explain, but I'm not so sure it made much sense to him. He wore his belt to daycare and made me promise to come and get him when the stuff stops falling."

"Mini you, I love it." Sharon threw pieces of deck boards onto the growing heap of old lumber. "Maybe he can come when we're putting the new one up."

"Okay, you bring Abs and we'll put Jimmy in charge of ball throwing. That should frustrate them both long enough to need a nap."

ৎ ৎ ৎ

With all parties on schedule, the old deck was down and cleared, the new lumber carried to the backyard, and the old loaded into the trailer by eleven.

"We are kicking butt today," Kasey remarked as Sharon heaved the last armful of boards to the top of the pile. "There something in the coffee this morning?"

"I don't know," Sharon replied, "but the world just feels so fresh and clean today. It's doin' wonders for my energy level."

Troy stifled a laugh, Kasey didn't. She removed her gloves and wiped her face with her forearm.

Sharon looked from one to the other. "What?"

"Fresh and clean missed your little part of the world," Kasey explained, laughing again at the layer of dirt and unidentified specks clinging to her clothes and sweaty skin.

"Ohh." Sharon pushed her shoulders back, lifted her chin higher than normal. "Well, some people can see the beauty deeper than that. I'm sorry you can't appreciate the inner place I'm in."

"Really? You think not?" Kasey retrieved her metal clip case from the front seat of the truck and returned to hand Sharon an envelope. "For the scholarship fund. I hit up everyone that I knew wouldn't have seen the website or your blogs. We wanted you to see them before Connie deposited them in the account."

"Wow, Kase," she said, examining check after check. "This means so much—"

"I know."

"Oh, no way," she exclaimed, pulling a check from the envelope. "You can't afford this, Kase." Then another check. "And neither can you, Troy. This is too much. I can't let you do this. We'll be fine without it."

"I can't speak for Troy, but—"

"Yes, you can," he said.

"Okay. This is important to us, too. It feels really good to do something so important in their names."

"Yeah, it does," Sharon replied. "Why did it take me so long to do this?"

"Why did it take any of us this long?"

Chapter Thirty

Breakfast had become a special time—healthy food for the body and healthy discussion for the soul. Laura looked hard at her mother. *Wiser than she ever knew, more beautiful than she could describe. Why had it taken a health crisis to get to this place?*

"Mom, do you think the same things that make you feel safe and secure are the same things that make you happy?"

"What has you so philosophical lately?"

"I've been enjoying being able to talk with you like this. Learning things about each other that we couldn't know in our mother-child life. It's different. It's a new kind of appreciation, and I'm so grateful that we have it."

"I loved the little girl that you were, my little helper. I couldn't believe how quickly you learned. I remember when you were ten and I came home from work and you had cooked a lasagna better than I could. I always knew that you would grow up and do something special with your life. There were times when you were growing up that I was even jealous of you, and now I'm just terribly proud of the woman that you are."

"Why would you be jealous? I was such a little know-it-all."

"You were smart and young and beautiful. You had all your choices still ahead of you, and I was living with mine."

"Then you did have regrets."

"Only after a rough day, or a lonely night. Most of the time I counted my blessings in your faces. Each of you were special in your own way—Jeannie my creative genius, Brett my problem-solver, Barry the athlete. Sometimes I couldn't believe how happy you all made me."

"Which brings me to my question."

"Having my family around me has always made me feel both safe *and* happy. But, you're asking for a broader answer, aren't you?"

"I wonder if I'm expecting too much in my own life. I'm starting to see trends that are disturbing, and choices that I'm afraid to make. Does what I see mean that happiness is relative? Am I giving up one to gain the other? And what if I really don't have a choice?"

"Oh, honey," Adele replied, "I hope you're not expecting me to have those answers for you. If you'll be more specific, I'll give you all the moral support I can, but I'm not going to have your answers for you."

"No. No one is going to have them for me. I just need to talk out loud, and have you add your thoughts and experiences, if that's okay."

"It's fine, honey. But don't expect any deep revelations from this old gal."

Laura offered a warm smile and the much-needed bottom line. "I can't get Sharon out of my head—"

"Heart. You can't get Sharon out of your heart."

"Well, don't wait so long to jump right in next time."

"Don't forget that you're the one who started this discussion."

"I'm sure you won't let me do that. And I do need you on the other end of this—while I talk some things out." Overdue things, their effective date probably expired, but needed nonetheless. "Do you think love trumps everything else?"

"If you're lucky enough to find it, I think it does."

"I've never stopped loving her. And I've never loved anyone like I love her."

"Have you given it a fair chance?"

"Years. Yes. I even tried being with someone who was as different from Sharon as I could find. Terese is socially refined, college educated, fashionable. But, you know what I realized attracted me to her? Her commitment, her passion to help the children. The same kind of over-the-top, no-holds-barred energy that attracted me to Sharon."

"But?"

"But I asked myself if she would have the same passion and commitment if she wasn't getting paid for it, and I couldn't be sure that she would. That's when I realized that I'm still comparing everything and everyone to Sharon. It's almost laughable. In fact, it would be laughable to Sharon. She could never imagine herself being compared to someone like Terese—favorably, that is. I can hear her laughing right now . . . that's part of her appeal, she has no clue that she's appealing at all. I miss that. I miss her honesty in who she is, and her sense of community. I feel like I've lost my own. I'm surrounded by straight colleagues and straight friends, and Terese is a very private lesbian. She has to be in order to do what she does so effectively. She doesn't get involved in our community or politics, and our relationship had to be kept behind closed doors. I found myself feeling isolated and even vulnerable sometimes."

"Does she know how you feel?"

"We talked about it off and on. I'm sure she was just waiting for me to decide what I could be happy with in my life. I'm equally sure that she was perfectly content for things to continue as they were. But, in our last conversation she made it clear that she knew I wouldn't be. She's a smart lady. She made it easy for me to tell her that she was right. I was surprised at how unemotional it was, and how relieved I felt."

"Maybe subconsciously you were protecting yourself because you knew it wasn't something that would last."

"Probably. It's amazing what you can learn about yourself when you're willing to pay attention."

"If only we can learn the important things early enough . . . so, this is probably where you expect some helpful advice from your mother."

"You taught me what I needed a long time ago, but I didn't realize it until recently. I was so fixated on the dysfunction that Dad's disease brought to our family that I couldn't see what it was teaching me about family. I know now that what's most important to Sharon is the same thing that I'm looking for."

"So, if you are still in love with her, what are you going to do about it?"

"I may not have a choice, Mom. I'm the one who left. Whether it was the right thing to do or not, doesn't change what is or is not possible now."

"Do you want her back in your life?"

A long hesitation, and then, "I do."

"Then try."

"And if she is single, and forgives me, and still loves me, but we just can't live together, then what? I don't know, Mom. I don't want to hurt her again."

"Why don't you let her decide?"

"Because I'm afraid that I know Sharon better than I know myself. She goes at everything full tilt. She focuses so hard on the goal that she doesn't realize when the means is literally destroying her. I've never forgotten a story that she told me about her brother because, whether she knows it or not, it describes her perfectly. They went to a small high school where getting the numbers out for athletic teams was most important, and cuts were virtually nonexistent. So, when the track team needed another hurdler, Sharon's brother stepped up. He was built like Sharon, too short and too thick to run hurdles. But that didn't stop him. He ran, and even won some, but he did it by hitting and knocking down every single hurdle with his shin. She said he was a bloody mess after every practice and meet, but he wouldn't quit."

"That's why you left, isn't it? You couldn't stop her from hurting herself. I get it now."

"She had to figure it out for herself, and I didn't know if she ever would. I loved her too much to stay and watch."

Adele waited, thoughtful, then, "I have to confess something to you."

Can you ever be prepared to hear a confession from your mother?

"You already know," Adele began, "how much I like Sharon. I did from the first day I met her and she spent all that time talking to me, and teaching me to play euchre. She always made me feel like she enjoyed having me around."

"She really did. There are no hidden agendas with Sharon. Good or bad, she's right up-front."

Adele nodded. "I like that."

"But that's no confession."

"No, but it was why it hurt me so to honor your wishes, and why I've resented you for asking me not to communicate with her. I ignored every card and letter from her. That was so hard to do, it about broke my heart."

It was beginning to make sense now. The obvious so overlooked in the struggle. "We both see Dad in her, don't we? That vulnerable soul trying to fight off its demons, and the undeniable sweetness there beneath it all—we want to see it win out this time, don't we?"

"Yes," Adele replied with a nod, "we sure do."

Chapter Thirty-One

The stresses of the workday, physical and otherwise, had been there as usual—late appointments, billing miscues, low blood sugar—but Laura handled them automatically. Her thoughts, buzzing through a sleepless fog, would not leave Sharon.

Throughout the day, and even now as she negotiated busy streets and malfunctioning traffic lights by rote, the battle with indecision and apprehension continued. Yet, despite the battle, the one thing that she was sure of had driven her on. *She loved Sharon Davis and, regardless of the consequences, she would tell her that, and then life, wherever it is meant to go, could go on.*

She hadn't noticed if there was a car parked in front, or if Sharon's truck was in the drive. She hadn't noticed that the grass was freshly cut and the porch railing now had bronze-colored iron spindles. She could only see how close she stood to the door, and wonder how long she had been holding her breath.

Exhale, breathe, knock. Her hand rapped the door, her mind went blank. She stared straight ahead, unwilling to knock again, unable to turn around. Moments later, the door opened.

The look on Sharon's face was surprise. Yes, she decided quickly, surprise. No hint of anger, no frown. And before Laura could stop them, the tears, and then the words she needed to say gushed forth. "I love you."

In the next moment she was in Sharon's arms, thick and strong—the embrace she remembered, comforting and reassuring. A place where all is right, even when it isn't.

The tears kept coming.

"Shh, baby, it's okay," Sharon whispered. "Everything's okay."

Tears wet Sharon's neck. Abby's kisses wet Laura's calves.

"I've missed you," Laura managed, "so much." Sharon's arms tightened around her, soft lips pressed the side of Laura's face.

"Don't cry, baby. Please don't cry. You're here now. It's gonna be okay."

Laura lifted her head, but made no attempt to focus blurred eyes. She concentrated on the words, the message she needed to hear, wanted to believe. It was going to be okay, she wanted to believe that.

Sharon's hands cupped Laura's face, turned it gently upward to bring Laura's lips to her own.

As gentle as Laura remembered. Tentative touches, asking, waiting. Answered as Laura returned the kisses—gently at first as the tears subsided. It was right to be here, to kiss her, to love her. It was okay to take now over then, and let the best of what was right between them breathe again.

"You're here," Sharon whispered. She kissed Laura's cheek and neck and shoulder. "I can't believe you're here."

The feelings were coming back, flashing and sparking, faster than she ever would have imagined. Worry and tears were gone, and in this moment she wanted nothing, hoped for nothing, but for Sharon to love her. She let her head drop back as Sharon pressed kisses to the sensitive skin of her neck. "Oh, yes," she said, closing her eyes. "I've missed you. I've missed you so much."

Laura grasped the back of Sharon's head, met her lips again, this time strong and sure. Whatever needed to be said, would be said later. She felt the familiar response, lips full and firm kissing her back, opened to them, answering back. She stood there, clinging to what she needed, letting the sensations build until her legs began to quiver.

"I can't," Laura breathed against open lips, "stand here much longer."

She'd made no conscious decision since the knock on Sharon's door. Her heart had sent her into Sharon's arms; her body, wanting and needing, took her to Sharon's bed.

The only words—"I love you"—gushed between them while hurried hands stripped away clothing and any doubt of intent. She wanted this love, this woman, this life. She wanted Sharon's hands to keep touching her, wanting her. She wanted the desire from Sharon's kisses to keep burning through her just as she remembered. Nothing else mattered—not fault or fear or time gone by—nothing except this moment and the desire taking her body.

Sharon's lips—full, insistent—told their passion better than words. They sought out all the sensitive places, touching them, remembering them, leaving a path of tingling warmth. *Oh, so warm. So wonderful.* "You make me feel so good." *Like no other lover.*

The lips had covered her body, lingering, languishing, pushing desire, stopping to engulf one hardened nipple, then the other. Passion teetered on the edge of patience—needing, wanting—but it felt so wonderful. Just a little longer, to let the sensations keep coming. Oh, to let the hands take their time over her belly and her thighs, to see how much heat she could take. *Please, just a little longer.*

But when fingers traced their first path through the wet heat, the edge she had held so precariously dissolved into the strongest need she had felt in years. With a gasp, Laura arched her back and pressed Sharon's mouth harder over her breast. "I need you now. Oh, baby, yes. Oh, yes. Oh, yes."

In the next instant, her body exploded in sensation. Wonderful, glorious sensation. And Sharon was inside her, moving with her, dissolving all possibility of thought, sending her body soaring into orgasm. No words, no thoughts. Just riding, rising, higher and higher, until there was no more air, no more breath. And yet, her body went on—spasms gripping, legs quivering, and Sharon's fingers gently stroking, stroking, coaxing still another spasm, and then another. Murmurs of love whispered across her chest, "so beautiful, so beautiful", and muffled into her neck, "whatever you want, baby. Yes, I love you." Then as kisses, so warm, gently trailed across her shoulder, the spasms weakened. Sensation softened into euphoria, and Laura relaxed into a gentle embrace.

"Oh, my sweet love," Laura whispered. "My sweet, sweet love."

Sharon lavished more soft kisses over the flushed skin of Laura's face and neck. "I love you, Laura. I love you more than I can tell you."

"Just keep showing me, honey. Don't ever stop showing me."

"I promise you. Give us this chance, and I promise you."

Laura touched her fingers to Sharon's lips. "No promises until you're sure." Laura could see the intensity in her eyes, sense the conviction. Could this be the conviction brought home, here where she had wanted it for so long? Dare she trust it? Give it the chance. Oh, yes, she could do that. "Until we're both sure."

"But, I know—"

"What we know for sure is that we both want to make love until we can't breathe—again and again, as long as we can."

When the warm lips touched her again, she knew Sharon understood.

ର ଓ ର

Movement on the bed woke Laura before Sharon could snuggle back in next to her. "Oh," she said, rising to her elbow, "what time is it?"

"Potty time," Sharon replied. "Someone really messed up Abby's schedule." She leaned and kissed Laura's neck. "That's 5:30 human time."

The kiss to Laura's neck was followed by another to her shoulder, and then another. Just that easily, desire came roaring back. Laura slid her hand under the soft cotton T-shirt. Her body relaxed as Sharon leaned closer, and their lips teased and promised.

"Mmm . . . no," Laura said, pulling back from what she knew would be deepening kisses, much harder to resist. "I've got to drive home, get a shower, and go to work."

Sharon nuzzled the warm place below Laura's ear. "Let's take the day off," she whispered, "and make love all day."

Laura dropped back onto the pillow and pulled Sharon into an embrace. She held her tightly and spoke softly. "How did we ever get anything done before?"

Sharon traced the outline of Laura's ear with the tip of her tongue. "Is that 'yes'?"

"Oh, God, honey. How do you keep doing this to me?"

"I don't know," she returned, adding a deep kiss to the crook of Laura's neck, "but, I plan to keep doin' it."

With both hands, Laura eased Sharon's head up to make eye contact. "No," she said as gently as she could, "not right now anyway." Sharon's eyes dropped away. "Even if I could take the day, have you thought about what would happen when Kasey found out why *you* didn't work today?"

Sharon sighed and rolled onto her back next to Laura. "You sure know how to douse the sizzle."

"Well, would you really want to go through that, when we could just meet for dinner and spend the evening together instead?"

"Could we have lunch together, too?"

Laura smiled and kissed Sharon's cheek. "Call me at lunch and let me know where you want to have dinner."

Chapter Thirty-Two

"What color truck does Kasey drive now?" Laura asked as Sharon rolled the truck to a stop at a busy intersection.

"A white Ford. But I'll spot it before you do." She glanced at Laura who was intently surveying the traffic passing through the light. "If I say 'duck,' just do it. Okay?"

Laura took a deep breath. "You should have let me cook dinner for us at Mom's."

Sharon smiled as the light turned green. "Come on, relax. Every time I saw this place advertised on TV, I thought of you. I never wanted to go there with anyone else, even though I knew it wasn't likely that I'd ever get a chance to take you there."

As Sharon returned her focus to the street, she reached out and took Laura's hand. "You know," she said, "if this is a cruel dream, I'm going to have to camp out in Dr. Talbot's office for a month." She squeezed Laura's hand. "But, you are here, aren't you? And I am taking you to that place . . . You're gonna like—"

Without warning, Laura dropped down on the seat. "In the left lane," she said. "Is that her?"

Sharon turned quickly as a white truck pulled even with them. "No. That's a Ram." After a check of her mirrors, Sharon caressed Laura's head and smiled. "All clear."

Laura sat up and exhaled an audible breath. "Well, *that* took me back years . . . decades, actually."

"A little adrenaline rush?"

"Riding around town in a car, making out with the most obvious

166

dyke in Bridgeport would have gotten me expelled from community college faster than if I'd gotten caught robbing a bank. I did a whole lot of ducking . . . then I transferred at the end of the year."

"You never told me about that."

"That first day that I saw you, organizing people for a Pride march, so visible and proud. I knew then that I never wanted you to think that I wasn't proud of who I was."

"I made you feel like that?"

"You did," she directed at Sharon's serious profile, "among other things."

"I never knew that, either."

"Maybe I shouldn't have told you. It's part of your appeal, you know."

Sharon turned with a smile. "Right up there with my buff body and charming wit, I'm sure."

"I swear you are my mother's daughter. She's not comfortable on the receiving end of a compliment, either."

"Hey, now," Sharon said, pulling the truck into a large paved parking lot. "Adele and I understand each other . . . and, we're here." She turned off the engine and turned to face Laura. "I hope this is as good as they said on TV. I really want this to be special for you."

"Honey, this place is going to be perfect—not because of how good the food is or how lovely the atmosphere is—it's perfect because you picked it especially for me." Laura touched her hand gently to Sharon's cheek. *Yes, it's there in her eyes, just as I remembered it. Need, wide open and honest, exposed to me, only me. That need to find the perfect, special bauble and shine it bright, then to find my smile reflected in it.* She placed a kiss to Sharon's lips. *She'll see it there. I'll make sure that she sees it there.* "Stop worrying," Laura said. "I'm going to love it."

൙ ൙ ൙

Sharon needn't have worried. The aroma alone, from the juices

167

sizzling on an outside grill and wafting through the parking lot, was convincing enough.

A soft glow filtered through a filigree of leaved branches arching over an old brick wall. Voices and laughter danced over the wall and harmonized with exotic strains of music, as the two found their way to the entrance of the Mongolian Fire Grill.

A host with a bright red shirt and a fresh college face greeted them at the door with menus and a smile. And, in case Laura had forgotten what it was like, Sharon rushed her back into the world of out-without-doubt.

"Reservation for Davis," she said. "I asked the woman when I called for a table outside. Something for a special lady on a special night."

It was a nice smiled he offered, no hint of disapproval or judgment. "I've got you covered," he said. "Follow me."

They passed through the inside dining area, and followed their host out along a bluestone path lined with waist-high stone walls. Varieties of hosta, planted along the top of the wall, provided privacy in blue and green and variegated stripes of yellow and white. As they walked, they peeked into the openings where the path veered off into little courtyards. In each one, diners were seated around large, flat, sizzling hot grills where their meals were being prepared.

Their host ushered them into a smaller courtyard with a smaller version of the grill they saw in the others, and pulled out their chairs. "Your waiter will be right with you. And your chef will be Lee Linn."

"Does he do what the chef in the commercial does?" Sharon asked.

Another smile from the host, just as genuine as the first. "He does. Actually, I think he's even better. You ladies enjoy your night," he said, as he left them alone.

Sharon's eyes shone in the soft light. "Wait 'til you see this," she said, her expression wide with childlike excitement.

There's something wonderful about that look—the unsophis-

168

ticated innocence of it, the far too few times in a person's life that they get to enjoy it. Laura took it in, cherished it, until the waiter appeared and then it was gone.

"Have you ever had Bantan?" Laura asked.

Sharon shook her head, "Not that I know of."

"It's a cream soup made with meat and dough crumbs."

"Not only a delicious soup," added their waiter, "but a favorite Mongolian hangover remedy."

"Okay," Sharon replied. "I don't think I'll be needing it for that, though."

"We'll both start with the Bantan," Laura continued. "And we'll also have the milk tea and some Boortsog."

"Very good," he said. "I'll be right back with your order, and bring out the raw bar for your chef."

"Boortsog?" Sharon asked as he left.

"Biscuits," Laura replied. "This place is the real deal."

"See, that was what made me nervous. I knew you'd know if it was the real thing or not. I didn't want to take you to some imitation joint."

"I would eat hotdogs with you at a hotdog stand if it put that same light in your eyes."

Sharon dropped her gaze for a moment. "I don't know what you see," she said, her gaze returning to Laura's.

"I'm not sure that I can explain it. It isn't just your eyes, it's the expression around them, too. It's like a brightness shining at me, like you are genuinely pleased that it pleases me."

"That *is* how I feel. I'm not one who would ever win a hand with my poker face. Good or bad, I don't hide it well."

"I wish I could hang on to that look. I tried hard over the years to find it again—not consciously—I didn't know for a long time what I needed to see, what I wasn't able to find. But, this is it, right there in your eyes. I think it must be the same look that my mother saw in my father's eyes. I think it's love."

"I do love you. I've kicked myself for a long time for not showing you like I should have." She closed her eyes for a second, then opened them to a thorough search of Laura's face. "But I'm not dreaming, am I? You are here, really here."

No, not a dream, Laura thought, absently thanking the waiter as he placed their food on the table. *This is real. As meant to be as a seaworthy ship finding her port. Haven't we weathered the storm, found our course?*

"Laura, this is really good." After a hesitant first sip, Sharon dove enthusiastically into her soup. "Really good."

"To be honest, I'm surprised that you chose this restaurant. There aren't a lot of choices for a meat and potatoes girl. When did you develop this culinary bravery?"

"A friend," she said, looking up. "Kim. We dated for a while. One of the ways that she amused herself was forcing me to eat all these strange foods with her. I swear she got more enjoyment out of my expressions than she did from the food."

"So, you gagged and fussed even when you liked it." A grin greeted her between sips of soup—the grin she had always envisioned having a yellow canary feather hanging out of its corner. "Why is it that I knew that?"

"Because the things that you know about me far outweigh the things that you don't know."

"I do, don't I?" She held Sharon's eyes, serious now, no mischievous glint. "You're wondering if that holds true for you, too. I'm pretty sure it does . . . there's a lot we need to catch up on, a lot we have to share with each other. But not right now, okay? Let's not let anything or anyone else share tonight with us."

Sharon nodded. "That still sounds like it's straight out of a dream. But, you know, I'm gonna stay right in it and hope I never wake up."

It was dreamlike, reappearing like this without warning, riding in on so much assumption. Dare we hope for the improbable, even imagine it?

She couldn't help watching Sharon, even as they chose from the raw bar, and the smell of the heated grill filled the air. She watched her as the chef cooked their dinner with a show of flashing knives, slicing and tossing, and coming dangerously close to clashing mid-air or lopping off a finger.

"Damn," Sharon exclaimed over the sizzle of the grill, "I'd have lost three fingers and cooked 'em up by now."

"That *is* amazing," Laura added, enjoying Sharon as much as she was the show.

This is the Sharon so few know, dressed in her new blue shirt and her best dress pants, all wonder and fascination. The Sharon behind the sarcastic quips, the wizard behind the protective curtain. My Sharon, trusting me with who she is and expecting no more than that in return.

In a final bit of fancy, a prawn exploded out of a volcano fashioned out of lamb and marmot, and landed precisely in the top of the chef's hat.

"Wow," exclaimed Sharon. "That was awesome. Do you ever miss?"

"Not often," he replied, quickly arranging the food on their plates. "Please enjoy your meals," he offered with a parting smile.

"Now there's gotta be some special insurance on that guy," Sharon said with a shake of her head. "He's damn good, isn't he?"

"Yes, he is. And, I'm hoping that you enjoy this meal as much as you did watching him prepare it."

"I'm gonna love it, because I'm here with a woman who's way too beautiful for the likes of me, who says that she loves me. How can I go wrong?"

Chapter Thirty-Three

Laura put the little soft-sided dog bed next to the extra pillow on her mother's bed, and pushed the doggie steps up to the side of the bed.

"Sharon's taking Abby out, so she'll be fine until morning," she said as Adele draped her robe over the foot of the bed. "Are you sure you don't mind Abby sleeping with you?"

"After two weeks, I'd have a hard time giving up my little sweetie. I miss her terribly when you guys don't stay here."

Laura kissed her mother's cheek. "She knew your name after the first couple of days that we were here. Now she watches when Sharon goes into the bedroom after work to see if clothes go into the green bag. And when they do, she launches into this hilarious celebration. She races up her steps to the bed, runs two tight circles, stops and pushes the top of the bag with her front feet, then down off the bed, down the hall, and back again to do it all over again. I'm guessing that she's pretty excited to see you, too."

Adele was smiling. "Everyone should feel so wanted . . . I'm blessed, and not just by Abby."

"You like having Sharon here, don't you?"

"I like having you both here, even if you are hiding out."

ভ ৩ ভ

Yes, it was their hideaway. Their place of total acceptance, of hope. A concentrated effort for the past two weeks to keep their relationship a secret, to give themselves a chance, to give passion free reign. Days of carefully guarded anticipation, capped by nights that explored the possibilities.

Tonight, like the other nights, when the bedroom door closed behind them, it shut out the doubt, the world of uncertainty. This was their time, exclusive and private. Sharon and Laura. Alone with their fire and their passion, with their wonder and hope. Lips and hands chasing need to its knees, only to have it rise up, stronger and more demanding, again and again. For a few hours each night, this was their world—short of air, white hot to the touch—and they didn't have to justify it to anyone.

There was no need to justify, or even talk, until the passion cooled and night turned to morning. Only then, with daily routines and responsibilities looming, did real talk begin.

This morning, Sharon began. She stopped toweling her wet hair and pulled the towel around her neck like a prize fighter. "You could not possibility have fit everything you own into this apartment."

Laura placed the last of her folded underwear in the dresser drawer. "Renting for years makes you keep everything to a minimum. You only have room for the things that you actually use. Mom had the tougher move—all those years in the same house."

"Does she wish she could have stayed in her house?"

"Not physically, there were too many stairs and too much upkeep. But emotionally, there were a lot of memories there . . . We split up the things that she wants to keep in the family, and gave away or sold what we couldn't move." Laura returned the empty laundry basket to the closet, and turned back to Sharon. "You know, I never realized how much had been left unfinished in that house until we emptied it. Bare lightbulbs, broken stair treads, kitchen linoleum half there, half torn out. We had just lived with it like that for years."

"And I was making you live the same way in our house."

"That had nothing to do with—"

"But maybe it did. You just said that you didn't realize it before.

I've been learning from the doc, about how we repress stuff—anyway, something got into me, and I felt all this extra energy to finish up the house. Doesn't it feel better to you, too?"

"Of course it does. You did a beautiful job."

"Hey," Sharon said, taking Laura's hands and pulling her toward her, "I have a great idea. Let's take Adele to see the house, it might make her feel as good as it does us. We could bring her over a couple times a week for dinner and maybe play some cards. It'll be good for her to get out and be in a different environment. What do you think?"

"I think I love you," she said, adding a kiss that lingered only long enough to assure that they would make it to work on time. "And I know Mother does."

"Ask her if she wants us to take her over tonight."

The sparkle of old, in her eyes, in her voice. Laura hated to chance dampening it. But, a bit of forethought now could avoid a flood later. "When are you going to tell Kasey?"

No response, other than a quick shift of focus.

"She's going to find out, one way or another . . . either you tell her, or wait until she sees us together somewhere or drops by the house when I'm there, and we have to endure another come-apart."

"Come on, admit it. It's kinda fun keeping it from her—keeping it from everyone. Parking next door, meeting here and places where we know none of them would ever go. It's kinda exciting, isn't it?"

The sparkle quickly morphed into an equally familiar glint of mischief. Laura adjusted her mind-set—like riding a bike, it comes back quickly.

"Don't you feel that scary kind of excitement," Sharon continued, "that excitement you felt when you and your first girlfriend were sneaking around to be together? Almost getting caught makes the next time that much more exciting."

"Blackmail's scary, too," Laura added with a smile. "My sister caught me making out with a girl behind our garage. I was in nonstop negotiations for hush payments, until I found her birth control pills. Suddenly, she was fine with cleaning the bathroom and washing out her own period underwear."

"Ooh, *that* was brutal. My brother and I were in on everything together, neither of us could have blackmailed the other. We did some great mischief together." A broad smile. "I had a co-worker once who was bent on gettin' me fired. You know, that poor woman's car just kept having problem after problem. Poor thing just couldn't seem to get to work on time."

"You should come with a warning."

"Admit it, this is kinda fun."

"It won't be so much fun when they find out what we've been doing. Kasey, for one, will take this personally."

"Yeah, I know . . . she's going to have to get used to the idea gradually. I've been dropping little bits every day about things we used to do, the good times we had years ago. I figure good feelings will start replacing the bad ones."

"So, a sit-down, heart-to-heart, confession/explanation isn't an option. Is that what you're telling me?"

"I feel like we're in this cool little rowboat, just you and me— well, we'll have to fit Adele and Abby in there, too—and I love our little boat. I don't want to do anything to rock it," she said, giving Laura the last kiss of the morning. "I don't swim well."

Chapter Thirty-Four

Funny thing about rowboats, they don't fare well in rough water. You can balance the load, pull with all your might to hold the oars steady, and yet a strong broadside wave can throw you in the drink.

It was all hands on board today to get their best property to date ready for sale. Close to schools and shopping, and easy access to I-94, the Madison Street house was a property that could defy the bad market. They had missed the most popular early summer moving period in order to get income from the rentals coming in, but they had kept the renovation costs down, and with no unforeseen disasters they should have it ready today.

Sharon had ripped out all the overgrown bushes and weeds along the front of the house, and was digging the holes for the new plants. Her helper for the day, Troy's son, Jimmy, headed for the door when he heard his dad call.

Minutes later, he was hauling a new gallon of paint down the driveway.

"Hey, Jimmy," Sharon called, "you need some help with that?"

He was his daddy's boy from the bottom of his Size 5 work boots to the top of his sandy brown curls. "No," he said with a strong lean and slow determined steps.

He was also Sharon's buddy. "Hold up, Jimmy," she said, hustling to the driveway. "I've got an idea." She had planned to do it herself, but this couldn't be more perfect.

"Here," she said, "put the paint right here beside the house, and follow me. This will be great."

Jimmy followed her to the truck, where Sharon pulled a bag from behind the seat. "Do you want to help me play a joke on your dad and Aunt Kasey?"

His expression was expected, wide-eyed, and delightfully mischievous. This wasn't their first escapade together.

She set the bag on the ground, and Jimmy peered in. Then he stuck his hand in, pulled it out and checked his fingers. "Wow," he exclaimed, "it looks real."

"Yeah, I think it'll fool 'em. Come on, let's hurry."

They scampered into the house and into the living room with its finely finished floor, and set their plan in motion. A minute later, Sharon was tucked around an inconspicuous corner and Jimmy's yells were echoing throughout the house.

Troy arrived first, racing in from the kitchen. "What? What? Are you all right?"

Kasey, almost tripping down the last steps, arrived breathless to find that Jimmy was fine, but a whole can of paint was pooling across the otherwise pristine floor.

"Oh, Troy, no," she cried. "Why did you have him try to carry something like that?" She threw up her arms and turned her head in frustration. "We were so close on this place."

Troy released his hug on Jimmy, who was barely able to keep from bursting into laughter. "I'm sorry, Kase. I'll clean it up. It might come up better than you think." He leaned closer over the spill, then reached down and touched. "Uh, Kase?"

She turned, distress still evident on her face.

"Take a closer look," he said, turning his attention to his son, who was squealing, "I got you, I got you!"

Kasey bent down and picked up the can, and the spill came with it. "Why do I fall for her sh—"

"You're gonna owe a quarter," Jimmy chanted to an arm-circling, hip-swaying dance move he learned from his favorite show.

"I guess that would be half a quarter," Troy said, cupping long fingers over the top of his head.

"Sharon!" Kasey yelled. "You going to let Jimmy have all the fun—or is it all the blame?"

Sharon emerged from her corner with a broad grin and a high five for her able accomplice.

"Proud of yourself?" Kasey asked.

"Hey, that's what you get for makin' a half-pint carry a gallon."

"Touché," Troy replied. "I'll get the paint myself."

"You're incorrigible." Finally a smile. "And sometimes even funny . . . so, can we get back to work now, please?"

ଓ ଓ ଓ

Clearly, stress isn't funny. Nor is injury or hate, or divorce. But humor, just as clearly, can magically loosen the tightness and anesthetize the pain. It had been needed—and missed—and its return was appreciated.

The day had gone smoother than most. Painting done, new fixtures installed, and landscaping finished. The house was done. The water calm.

Troy and Jimmy had done their share of clean-up and gone home. Sharon swept the last errant shreds of mulch off the sidewalk and into the flower bed. Kasey locked the front door, but instead of her usual "See you in the morning" on her way to her truck, she dropped her tool belt on the top step and sat down.

Kasey's voice, the expected wave beneath the boat. "How long did you think you could keep from telling me?"

Sharon gathered the shovel and rake together with the broom, and carried them to the back of her truck, then lifted Abby into the front seat.

Kasey waited.

Sharon surveyed the house, the yard, enjoyed the satisfaction. She needed to. Then she joined Kasey on the step. "Connie thinks we could afford to pick up a foreclosure before we sell this?"

No eye contact, only Kasey staring at Sharon's profile. "I don't even know what to say," Kasey said.

How about, "Why couldn't you just tell me?" or "You're a damn knucklehead"? I'd take that, if only that were the worst of it.

"You start having all these errands that have to be run during lunch breaks, you're rarely home in the evenings, and now practical jokes . . . and all those little 'remember whens'—you might as well have taken a bullhorn and announced it to the city. But you just couldn't tell *me*."

"What do you want me to say?"

"How long have we known each other?"

"Forever."

"So after all these years and all that we've been through together, our friendship doesn't deserve your honesty."

"No, I mean, yes, of course it does. But, I knew this was—"

"What you *should* know is that I care about you like family, that I just want you to be happy." Kasey grabbed her tool belt and stood. "And I think you know it might not be possible with Laura." As she left the steps, she added, "*That's* why you couldn't tell me."

Chapter Thirty-Five

Are you smarter the second time around? It sure seems logical that you would be. Sharon threw the ball again for Abby while she waited for Laura. No need for her to park around the block now, Laura can park in the drive right where she belongs.

So, why, if history tends to repeat itself, and people repeatedly make the same bad choices, does that still seem logical? You know what works and what doesn't, what makes you happy, don't you? Or, is love the exception, as blind as justice should be?

Another throw. So much energy.

But, love should be blind—like dogs loving their humans. They don't see ratty, old, out-of-fashion T-shirts or extra pounds. They don't care if you have a bad hair day or a wart the size of a quarter. All they know, all they care about is that you hug 'em and take care of 'em, and love 'em. That's it. And in return, they love you back with every minute they have with you. It's just like Danny said. He told her, Abby showed her. Almost losing Abby had added the exclamation point—you must cherish every minute. And a second chance with Laura? Yep, she'd cherish every single minute.

Abby heard the car before Sharon did. Ears up, ball forgotten, she raced to the edge of the drive and back again. She was using her new vocabulary, a series of short not-quite-barks, to announce that Laura was here. Sharon followed her to the side of the house.

"I have a new doorbell," Sharon said, feeling the familiar

twinge of excitement at the site of Laura, and watching Abby dance upright until Laura picked her up.

"The cutest doorbell I've ever seen." She nuzzled a greeting, accepted wet kisses in return, and released an excited, wiggling Abby on the ground again.

Sharon smiled. "Sometimes you just have to smile and accept that you're second fiddle."

Laura shook her head. "Abby's special, but you are not second fiddle." She reached for Sharon's hand. "I'm assuming they all know now."

"Oh, I'm sure."

She pulled Sharon into an embrace. "I can't tell you how good this feels."

Sharon held her tightly and nodded against her head. "I don't want to lose you again."

For the moment hearts beat hard—hope and promise and celebration—holding tight until Abby's circles and pleading could no longer be ignored. "We'll have to wear her out if we're gonna have any privacy." Sharon took Laura's hand. "Come on, we can talk and keep her from having a nervous breakdown at the same time."

They settled in old wicker chairs, given new life with a coat of paint and clean cushions, and let Abby have her way. "Oh, honey, look at the asters. Don't you just love the colors? They're even more brilliant than I remembered."

"They're beautiful. But I think I might have lost a few out front. I sort of let it get out of hand, and when I tried to clean up the beds I had a hard time remembering what was what."

"We'll get some more. As long as we get them in before the ground freezes, they'll be fine next year."

The words had begun showing up more often—"we," "us"— glints of gold sprinkled through their conversations. Sharon noticed them, thought about them. "Next year," did she mean "us" next year? For one of the rare times in her life, Sharon held her tongue, held the question and the need for immediacy. This was too good right now, the feeling of "us" again. She wouldn't chance losing that feeling, not today.

"I'm sorry I didn't do a better job keeping your garden," she said instead. "I thought of you, I saw you in my mind, taking care of it and admiring it. I know the changes by heart, how the whole color scheme is different each season. But I barely touched it. I don't know why. There are so many things I'm sorry for—the anger, and the drinking, ignoring you like I did, taking you for granted—I'm sorry for it all. And I'm trying to understand it, I really am. I'm going to Dr Talbot," she said, eyes sealing the promise. "And I *am* learning." A look away, another throw for Abby. "Mostly that I'm a stubborn ass with tunnel vision."

"I have a theory for why you do that."

"Do what?"

"Nail *yourself* to the cross." The expected puzzled look. "If you hit yourself first, and hard enough, then no one else will bother trying. Right?"

The next throw was held up in thought. Abby took the opportunity for a breather and a drink. "And I'm giving Dr. Talbot my money?"

"Rightfully so, it's only a theory. You're doing the right thing, honey. It looks like we've both been busy learning a lot that we didn't know about ourselves."

"That's going to help us this time, isn't it?" Sharon locked her gaze on the grey-blue eyes. "I want this to work this time, more than anything."

"If it wasn't helping, we certainly wouldn't be sitting here together right now. But, I don't personally know anyone else who would be sitting where we are, so we're on uncharted ground—we're on our own to figure this out."

"Ya think?"

"I think it's a blessing. No one to draw false hopes from, or advice to wade through. We're right where we needed to end up—looking at what brought us back together, and what will keep us together."

"Love—we love each other."

"We loved each other before, too," Laura said. "But it didn't keep us together."

"Then, what did bring you back?"

"What I've learned about love . . . now I know that love is stronger than hate, stronger than fear, and that it's the only thing that can truly keep a family together."

Sharon nodded. *Such a simple thing. Leave it to Laura to learn the important stuff.* "I've learned that I'm not an alcoholic," she offered. "I thought I was—well, you and probably everyone else thought I was, too. But, I'm not. Doctor Talbot helped me sort it out. My body doesn't crave it, my mind does. Anyway, so working on my head is making a difference." Abby gave up on another throw and jumped onto Sharon's lap. "Not a life-changing revelation, but it helps me to know."

"It helps us." Laura reached over and stroked the back of Sharon's head. "I was prepared," she continued, "to face the fact that you were alcoholic. I spent a lot of time making sure that I wasn't following in my mother's footsteps. I wasn't going to waste my life trying to live with an alcoholic, no matter how much I loved her. And then, I fell in love with you."

Sharon broke eye contact, and stroked a sleeping Abby. Yes, she had told her that—more than once. The message, though, had blurred right along with everything else. She hadn't understood it then, and was embarrassed to now.

Laura's eyes had settled on the garden. Vibrant lavenders and purples defied their earth-bound vulnerabilities, clustered, and held strong. They'd shed their showy blooms with a promise, and kept it through the freeze of winter. "I thought I hated my father," she said, eyes distant. "And when you drank, I could smell him on you—the disappointment, the unkept promises—and I didn't want to hate you. I didn't want to hate him. I thought love should be clear and obvious, that I should be able to see it in order to count on it. Others should be able to see it. Dad should have been there in the front row seat, reserved just for him, when I won the spelling bee. He should have heard my salutatorian speech and been the favorite choice to chaperone the senior dance . . . But, you know," she said, bringing her eyes to Sharon's, "love is actually more like a perennial—always there below the surface. Not always showy and beautiful, but there, with its roots, resilient and strong, sunk deep in the soil. I know that now, too late to share it with my father, but hopefully not too late for us."

"Why do you say hopefully?"

"Because I'm not taking anything for granted this time, and because we have an uphill battle we didn't have the first time."

"Kasey," Sharon added.

"All of them. They're your family, and I need them to be my family, too."

"Hey, it's gonna be okay. They're tough, especially Kasey, but they'll be fine. We're not asking them to live with us."

"I hope you're not being overly optimistic."

"Abby and I had been thinking about hosting a card night. I won't be embarrassing myself now that I have most of the finishing done on the house, so maybe this would be a good time to jump in with both feet. What do you think?"

"Something about that makes me think of my mother throwing all of us kids in the same room when my brother got chicken pox. The thinking was 'Let's not spread this torture out any longer than we have to. Let's get it over with right now,'" Laura frowned. "Do mothers even do that anymore?"

"I don't know. Someone would probably turn them in to CPS . . . So, you're saying card night's not a good idea?"

"I'm wondering if the alternative, facing them individually or as couples, would be even less comfortable. Would they be more, or less, likely to show how they feel in a group?"

"From what you told me about your talk with Connie, I'd say that she's our strongest ally. Having the rest of them there won't change that. Sage will figure that it's none of her business, and Deanne's very hard to read."

"And we both know where Kasey stands."

"I'm going to let you make this decision. Pox or no pox?"

Laura traced her fingers lightly through the hair above Sharon's ear. She tilted her head and waited, wondered if she really should be the one to make this decision. After a sigh, she replied, "I say pox. Take my hand, Thelma."

Chapter Thirty-Six

"No interruptions for the next hour," Sage directed the secretary stationed just outside her Longhouse office. "Except for Deanne. Direct everything to Wendy, even if they ask for me. Thanks, Diane," she said, retreating to her office and closing the door behind her.

She was under no illusion that her company couldn't run just fine on its own. Wendy was as competent a manger as there was, and with a hand-picked staff, there were no real worries. But Sage needed to feel the pulse, the living breathing pulse of her retirement community. More than a business, it was a promise, made and kept, to honor her grandmother. And she needed to feel it, to smell it, to see it. A direct connection, direct control.

It wasn't so easy, though, to keep her finger on the pulse of her family. The beat and breath that mattered so much was so far away. A constant test of her spirit, of her belief that all is connected and works in harmony if you allow it. If only she had her grandmother's strength of spirit, her trust in what can only be sensed. Sage tried to listen, to stay open to the signals. But always at the end of the day it came down to deciding what to act on, how hard to push. The one thing never in doubt was that she would do whatever she could to make her family whole.

Sage stood at the large office window overlooking the koi pond a few yards away. Its location there was strictly by design. She loved the tranquility of it, counted on the gentle flow of water over the large flat rock to slow her heart rate, and allowed her thoughts to follow the effortless glide of the koi. It tempered the sense of helplessness, and made room for solution. Lessons from nature.

She would learn them, as her grandmother had taught her. And if she listened long enough, well enough, she would find the healing. It's what she wanted most, for herself and for her family, a way to heal. And, knowing now that that was possible was proving harder to accept than having no hope at all.

Fading rays of sunlight played tag with a koi and slithers of orange and white. Sage breathed deeply and waited for Jeff's call.

CЯ CƷ CЯ

It was time to fulfill the promise that he had made to himself. And today, Jeff decided, while Cimmie spent the evening with Lena, was the perfect opportunity. He and Naline would have their talk.

"Hey, Naly," he called, "come help me decide what to fix for dinner."

"Just a minute."

Jeff left the kitchen to peer in the doorway of Naline's room. "Where are you?"

"I'm making a surprise for you in here," Naline called from her parents' bedroom.

He stopped short of the bedroom door and asked, "Is it okay to come in?"

There was a short hesitation, and then, "Okay, come in."

Naline stood in the middle of the room holding a white paper sign in front of her and a proud smile on her face.

"What is this?" Jeff asked, noting a white sign on every piece of furniture in the room.

"Seneca words. See, I put the words on everything so it will be easier." She pointed to the bed and the sign taped to the head-board. "Kano'skwa'," then to the sign on the back of the chair, "Katsi'kaya'. Ben said that children learn best, but I said that you're really smart, and he thinks you aren't too old to learn."

Jeff couldn't contain a laugh. He looked from sign to sign, put his hands on his hips, and nodded. "Well, I guess I have my work cut out for me. I sure don't want to let you or Ben down."

Naline took the sign she was holding and put it on the door, then took her dad's hand. "It will be special, like you said it was when you were growing up with Uncle Aaron and you made up your own sign language."

"It was special. And, you know what, even though that was a long time ago, I'll bet he and I could still talk to each other across the room and no one would even know it."

"Do you miss Uncle Aaron?"

"Uh, huh, I do." He squeezed Naline's hand. "Hey, let's go out to the kitchen and talk about some things. Okay?"

She kept his hand and led him down the little hallway. As soon as they were comfortably settled at the table, soda and trail mix at hand, he began. "I've been doing some thinking about something important."

"Okay. Is it a secret?"

"No, we'll talk about it with Mom when she gets home, too." Naline was sipping her soda, but her eyes were focused intensely on her father. "If we could make a plan so that you and Mom and I could move to Michigan and you could go to school with Cayley, would you want that?"

"Yes, yes, yes," she said, bouncing up and down on her chair. "Can I tell Cayley? Can I call her right now?"

"Wait, Naly. I know this sounds really exciting, but I want you to think about all that moving would mean first. Okay?"

"I know, we'll get lots of boxes and I'll help wrap everything in newspaper like when we moved Grandma Lena."

"I know you'll be a big help, but there's more to think about than just packing. For your mom and me, it means we will have to leave our jobs and try to find jobs there so that we can pay our bills and make a new home for us. And, for you, it will mean leaving your friends and your school, and not getting to see your grandma and Ben and Sarah as often."

Naline relaxed against the back of her chair, thoughtful for a moment. "Did you ever move?"

"Uh, huh," he replied with a nod. "A couple of times."

"Did you miss your friends?"

"I did. Especially when I was in high school and I was on the wrestling team. It was really hard to leave my teammates. But I always made new friends."

"And you always had Uncle Aaron."

"Right up until he got married and moved to California. He was always my best friend."

"Cayley is *my* best friend."

"So, what say you, Naly? Do we move?"

"Yes!"

❧ ❧ ❧

There had been no sense in trying to do any paperwork, and the waiting had finally sent Sage outside to sit at the edge of the koi pond. She was fighting the temptation to call Jeff when the phone rang.

"I want to apologize for taking so long," Jeff began.

"Not a problem, Jeff, I needed the break today."

"Not about today. I'm apologizing for taking so long to understand how important this move would be for the family. I've been assessing this whole thing through my traditional family experience, even though I prided myself on being such a progressive thinker."

The relief had already begun to set in. There was even a trace of a smile on Sage's face. "I'm not sure there is another man, Jeff, who would have knowingly walked into this family situation. I respect that, and I do understand that this hasn't been an easy decision."

"It came down to really seeing how completely opposite your family experience is from mine. How mine developed as expected. Children grew up together under their parents' care until they matured and moved out. Then they found careers and got married and started the process all over again . . . But you and Cimmie never experienced family that way. I started to see your need to pull together a family that wasn't there when you were growing up. But when I had my talk with Naline today, she put it all into one simple sentence. When she said, 'Cayley is my best friend,' I got it. I was able to grow up with my best friend. But Cimmie wasn't, and now Naline. And you've been right all along. This is where we stop the cycle, Sage, right now."

The feeling, growing and sparking and filling her now, was so unexpected. Sage drew a deep breath and shuddered in exhale. This kind of excitement had never been allowed. The lesson that it would only be squashed, had been learned early and never forgotten. The only way to keep something this good was to mask it. But, it did indeed feel good. She cleared her throat. "You know," she said, and cleared her throat again, "we've both been wrong in thinking that what *we* thought mattered most. That the decision to move or not depended on *our* assessment of what is best. It shouldn't have been ours at all."

"No. We have too much clouding our vision. The children see things so clearly and simply."

"Have you told Cimmie yet?"

"She's at Lena's. I'll tell her, well, I'm sure it will be Naline telling her the minute she walks in the door."

"And Lena? Should we leave it up to the girls to talk her into moving, too?"

"I think that's the best plan I've heard in some time."

ଔ ଔ ଔ

"*Well,*" Deanne said as she made her way along the stepping stones, "I like *that* expression. That is so much more than 'I am glad to see you right now.'" She walked directly into Sage's embrace and kissed her firmly.

"Oh," Sage replied when their lips parted, "but I *am* glad to see you. Always. Every day."

"Yes," she said, "but what brightened you before I even got here?"

"I just talked with Jeff."

Deanne leaned back. "And?"

Sage let her hands rest at the small of Deanne's back. "You know the talk we had with Cayley regarding school and how we listened to what she needed and wanted, how we took that leap of faith? Well, he had a talk with Naline, just the two of them, without Cimmie."

"They're coming to Michigan."

The excitement in Deanne's voice made Sage smile.

"Yes," Sage replied softly. She pulled Deanne to her again, snugged her arms around her, and kissed her head. "Not tomorrow, but yes."

ભ ભ ભ

The grounds of the Longhouse were stunning this time of year—meticulously groomed greens and glorious displays of summer annuals. The light sweet scent of fragrant tea olive blossoms lifted from the bushes lining the wide walkway that wound past the main buildings. Deanne waited until they split from the walkway and headed toward the cottage before she took Sage's hand. A courtesy, unspoken, understood—the residents could sense their commitment, but they didn't need to see it. A compromise of sorts; for Sage, there were few things in life that warranted that particular discretion. But, the Longhouse was not her home, it was her business—a place where professionalism and respect were meant to go hand in hand.

Sitting just beyond the center hubbub of the Longhouse and tucked into a niche of tall white pines, the cottage was picture-perfect—and empty. Sage made a quick outside assessment as they crossed the little cedar porch with its rough-sawn posts, then surveyed the inside room by room.

"For now, I've got a one-bedroom apartment that will be perfect for Lena." Sage said as she rejoined Deanne in the hallway. "This will be hers later, after I've had time to talk Jeff and Cimmie into a house on the lake."

"They won't accept you building them a house as a gift."

"I know . . . come with me tomorrow to pick out some furniture for this place?"

It didn't seem to matter how long she had known Sage, there was always something that rose to the top of awareness, formerly unrecognized, unappreciated. No open book, this woman. No ordinary childhood where growing up followed the normal learning curve. How she got from there to here might never be understood.

"You were sure, weren't you?" Deanne asked. "Having Kasey build this place, but not renting it. Somehow you knew, didn't you?"

"I never *know* as my grandmother would have known," she replied. "I just tried to trust as she would have expected me to. The rest was hope."

"I'd say that you did a little more than hope. A lot of planning, worrying, your struggle to remain patient." She locked onto the serious brown eyes. "Your anxiety and worry I understand, but I don't know how you contain it so well."

"I've had a lot of practice. If you slip past containment you fail, and in my growing up years, failure was never an option. The result was too costly."

"Having the family here, all present and accounted for, is going to be such a huge relief . . . It just occurred to me that I've never known you without that stress and worry."

"I can't remember a time without it."

Deanne reached up and slipped her arms around Sage's neck. "Then, I'd say that it's about time someone lightened the load." She kissed her gently, lovingly. When Sage's hands moved over her back and their kiss deepened, it was easy to imagine a night of celebration. It was a worry-free Sage Bristo that was nearly impossible to imagine.

"I want that for you," Deanne whispered, as their lips parted. "No worries." She laced her fingers through the back of Sage's hair. "Except the occasional school notice regarding our precocious daughter."

A smile turned the corners of Sage's mouth only briefly before the cell phone on her waistband sounded. She quickly read the text message, and her smile widened. "Connie. She wants to know if Cimmie will come for a job interview."

"Perfect, perfect."

There was slightly less excitement in Sage's voice. "It doesn't mean that she's a lock for the position. I don't know how much influence Connie has in the matter. I'm sure it will be a relief if Cimmie gets it, but she'll have time to find something else if she has to. And Jeff can take whatever time he needs to get his Michigan teaching certificate."

"Maybe you can talk with Connie tomorrow night about it. Do you think she and Kasey will show up at Sharon's, or do you think because of Laura . . .?"

"I called Kasey yesterday and told her that I think it's important for her to be there. I have no doubt that Connie would show up alone, but Kasey is as stubborn as Sharon is." She tipped her head with a slight shrug. "I guess we'll see tomorrow."

Chapter Thirty-Seven

Abby greeted each of them, including Kasey, first with tail wags that put her whole body in motion, then standing on her hind legs to be sure that she received her full measure of attention. Which, of course, they all gave, partly because friendly cute little dogs are easy to love, and partly because attention spent on Abby made the limited attention given to Laura less noticeable. Or, so they hoped.

Brief "hellos" and quick smiles, a warm hug from Connie, and just that quickly the most politely tensioned card night any of them had experienced was under way.

The familiar basement, once sporting beer signs and bar knick-knacks, now proudly displayed framed pictures of Grethe Cammermeyer and Eleanor Roosevelt and Gloria Steinem and Martina Navratilova on its walls. The door to the little kitchenette was gone and the space opened into the large room. Snacks and plates and glasses, and all the necessities of a properly hosted evening were readily available on the counter, and served as easy distractions to the less than comfortable reunion.

"Okay," Sharon announced, "Six people tonight, round-robin euchre. So, someone from each couple take a number from the bowl on the table here, and we'll see who plays who first. Since we're just getting started again and playing only once this month, we'll play the best of three and each couple will play the others twice. Winner at the end of the night gets dinner wherever they choose."

The numbers drawn put Kasey and Connie against Sage and

Deanne, and granted Laura a much-needed buffer of time to allow palpable tension to dissipate. Choose your words carefully, she reminded herself, and give it time. If there was a better way, she had no idea what it would be.

Little Abby was *her* shield now, lovingly snuggled against her chest—a soft and impenetrable barrier that no one dare violate. Not Deanne, the calmer of waves, shifting, uncomfortable with her expected repulsion. Or Sage, welded tight, all compression fittings securely in place. The deep unknown, the keeper of secrets. And surely not Connie, sitting there so sure of her logic, watching players on a stage. Not even Kasey would violate the barrier—not physically. The fuse would never ignite violence, only shoot charged warnings from her eyes; a shame, really, soft blue so steely now.

Tonight, survival would be a state of mind. Laura chose a bar stool next to Sharon, and took a deep, slow breath.

The atmosphere was far from that of the card nights they used to have, filled with teasing and laughter. And in the absence, subtle nuances flashed in neon.

Kasey's eyes denied access, focusing only on the cards or on Connie, even when someone else was speaking.

"Get good and warmed up," Sharon advised form her stool. "I don't want any whining when we kick your asses."

The only response was a smile from Connie, and "You're such a kidder," from Sage. The cards continued sliding, one on top of the other, and the points began to add up. The first game, won by Sage and Deanne, led to the next and the cards from Kasey's hand came quicker and slid farther across the table.

"Did you have to play that one?" Connie finally asked in frustration. "I already had the hand."

"Does it matter?"

Connie's glance at Deanne proved nothing was being missed. "Only if you care whether we win or not."

No response. Only the last of the cards down and the points and game to Sage and Deanne.

Kasey stood abruptly. "All yours," she said in Sharon's direction.

Sharon ignored the tone. "Come on," she said, motioning to Laura. "Someone needs some serious ass-kickin'—but we'll start with these two."

"We're talking about cards here," Deanne said, "aren't we?"

"Yeah, cards," Sharon replied, settling in the chair across from Laura. She pushed the deck to her partner and added, "Deal, my lady."

And deal she did. Cards good enough to carry the first hand. And when their luck held, the win had them smiling at each other like giddy schoolgirls.

"One in the win column," Laura said with a wink. Yes, school's out, tests taken, pressure's off. We're skipping home, spirits helium high and nothing else matters.

Sage handled the deck with one hand, long fingers splitting it, reforming it. "Consider that our version of the Welcome Wagon," she said, dealing the cards almost unnoticeably. "But one win out of three is all you'll get."

She was right. Cards played and fell, and the points eluded Sharon and Laura. Two quick games, two quick losses, and with the helium totally gone now, they were elbow to elbow with Kasey and Connie.

In the background, Gladys Knight's man was catching the midnight train to Georgia, while Sharon was unable to stop her eyes from meeting Kasey's. She waited on them, silently wishing for their mercy, their usual compassion, their understanding.

Instead she got, "Don't expect any welcome wagon here."

. . . he's goin' back to find what's left of his world . . .

"Then what about offering a little forgiveness," Sharon replied. "That would go a long way in cutting through this damn tension."

. . . I'd rather live in his world . . .

"It's okay, Sharon," Laura said, "let it go." Words more futile than she remembered.

"Didn't we learn this lesson years ago?" Sharon forced a hard look from Kasey, straight-on, stripped-down way past pretense. "I put us through this once, with Connie, and I've owned that mistake. We both know how important forgiveness is."

"Do we?" Kasey ignored a *Leave it alone* look from Connie and continued. "Or is it that we demand forgiveness only when we need something from it?"

"What are you talking about?"

Kasey cocked her head. No one tried to silence her. "You can't be so pious about expecting forgiveness from others when you can't give it yourself."

"You wanna spell that out?"

Connie stood. "We should go, Kasey."

Kasey waved away Connie's hand. "Crawford?"

Sharon stood abruptly, almost pushing her chair over. Her eyes bore hard. "You actually said that. My best friend with the nerve to say that—here in my own house."

"That's why I can say it. There may be others thinking the same thing, but probably thinking that it's not their place to say anything." Sharon looked stunned. "I'll work on how I feel about Laura, you know I will. But you have no intention of doing anything about how you feel about Crawford. Even though the anger tears you up, you see no reason, no justification to change."

Sharon leaned forward, bracing herself by planting one hand on the top of the table. "That's *not* the same thing." She pressed her finger against Kasey's chest. "You *know* in there it's not."

The room had frozen around them, no one moving, no one talking, music only a muffling as it seeped into the walls. The unrelenting stare was broken only when Laura rose from her seat. She stretched her arm across the front of Sharon's body and coaxed her back from the table.

"That's right, I don't see any justification—"

"Come on," Laura said, "let it—"

"Because there isn't any—none."

Kasey's voice rose slightly. "You're not hearing it the way I meant it." She held up her hand and left her chair.

"I think what she meant," Connie added, "was justification for *you* to change, not justification for what Crawford did."

"It doesn't matter," Kasey said. "It's not important."

"It is important," Connie continued, "because it's about Sharon, and your concern for her. That's what this is really all about. So we all need to take a breath and calm down."

"Since when is my welfare everyone else's concern?"

Sage shook her head. "You don't really need an answer to that, Sharon."

Deanne finally spoke. "Why don't we take this down a couple of notches and actually have a discussion. I just realized that, as a group, we've never discussed how the murders affected us. Each of us has dealt with it on our own, and probably with our partners, but never as a group."

"I'll tell you right now that there won't be a consensus of opinion," Kasey said. "That's why we've all dealt with it individually."

"I don't care if there's a consensus or not." Sharon walked clear of Laura and began a slow, methodic circling of the room. "No one else," she said with a thump to her chest, "has to live inside here."

"Thank God," Kasey replied.

"Kase," Connie warned.

"Yeah, well. I'm not wishing it on anyone anyway. It's not usually a pretty sight." She reversed her circle. "I got no illusions about that. So, consensus or not, it makes no difference to me."

"As I was saying," Deanne began. "I don't know how anyone else feels, except Sharon. Agree with her or not, she's the only one who leaves no doubt where she stands . . . Now that I think about it, I'm not quite sure how I felt about the whole Crawford release thing. Sometimes I find myself pushing things aside when I know that I don't have to make the decision. That's exactly what I did—my lazy way of dealing with a tough issue."

"See," Sharon said, raising her hands, "now I don't understand how that's a tough issue. He's guilty, he got life, he paid with every second of it. Period."

"But, it's not about him," Kasey added. "At least, it shouldn't be. As long as we're talking about him, angry at him, arguing over him, we're giving him power to make our lives miserable. Is that what Evonne and Donna would want?"

"It does go beyond him," Sage replied. "But he's a catalyst, a call to action that can't be ignored."

"No one's going to argue the importance of a strong political stand," Connie said. "But a personal stand is important, too. Each of us has our own measure of justice—the level we're comfortable with, when we feel that everything is as right and just as it can be. I have to say I'm with Sharon on this one. I can forgive rudeness, I can turn the other cheek to ignorance, but I can't forgive evil. I need to know that he paid the highest price possible."

"And what is a price high enough?" Kasey asked. "Is there one high enough to keep the anger from eating all the joy out of your life? Or high enough to keep you from spending precious chunks of your life thinking about horrible things in the past, instead of looking for good things in your life? What price are you paying then?"

Laura, hesitant until now to offer an opinion, finally joined the conversation. "You're right, Kasey. It's too high a price." She avoided Kasey's eyes, widened in surprise, and concentrated on Sharon. The motion of Sharon's head, back and away, told Laura what she feared. She was seeing this as a sign of betrayal. "I see patients every day who are dealing with loss, physical loss, but I think the comparison can be made. They need to heal physically just as we all need to heal emotionally. They have to use every ounce of energy to battle back and gain the strength to reach their new potential, sometimes even beyond. And they can't do it if they waste energy looking back at what they lost. Hate and anger, and even sadness take away precious energy from healing. They have to move their focus ahead. Instead of focusing on what they can no longer do, they have to focus on what can be."

"I *have* been working on what can be," Sharon replied. "A

Hate Crimes law will go a long way toward putting things right in the future. But, there's no way I'm going to forgive and forget."

A more compassionate tone this time from Kasey. "Forgiving doesn't mean forgetting, Sharon. You can work toward justice without vengeance. What difference does it make if Crawford died at home in his bed or in a prison hospital? The important thing is that a murderer was brought to justice, and his crime now has a name. Wouldn't you have just been punishing his family at this point? What would that have accomplished? Don't you think they have suffered too?"

"I'm thinking about the message that letting him go home would have sent, that's what I was thinking about."

"What message?" Kasey asked. "Compassion maybe?"

"Yeah, I've got compassion, and it's right where it needs to be."

"Is that the same compassion that—"

"Come on, Kasey," Connie interjected, "please drop it."

Kasey refused. "But, hasn't anyone heard what Laura said?"

Sage, detached and mostly silent on the night, finally spoke from the bar stool against the wall. "I heard her, I've heard what everyone had to say. I'm just wondering how any of you can tell someone else what they need to do to heal."

Silence from the women. Only glances, one to another, as the music continued in the background.

"How many of you have felt hate, cold steel hate, pressed against your flesh? Hate so close to you that you can smell its stench, so powerful that you know that any moment it could take your last breath?" She pulled the collar of her shirt aside to reveal the beginning of a white jagged scar. "It leaves scars. Some visible, identifiable. But others have marked you deep in a place you can't touch. You can't will them away, or medicate them away; sometimes you can't even find them. But they're there—forever. And forgiveness?" Sage shook her head. "Doesn't take them away."

Deanne moved to stand closer to her, and slipped her fingers through the half-turned curls above Sage's ear. Only music compromised the silence. No one spoke.

Sage continued. "So no one can tell me who to forgive or what to forget—and you can't tell me how—anymore than I can tell you, or you," her eyes met Kasey's and Laura's, "or Sharon. It's personal. It's deep. If you're lucky, it's contained. And if everyone else is lucky, it becomes fuel to accomplish things that we never thought we could."

Sage stood and pulled her keys from her pocket. "Someone has to carry the fire in their belly," she said, stopping to extend her hand to Sharon. "Carry it well."

Chapter Thirty-Eight

The basement was quiet once again. Card night aborted.

"She was right," Laura began. Sharon turned from collecting glasses from the table.

"Sage," Laura continued, "she's right about you."

"Yeah, well, why did she have to be right *tonight,* right in front of you? And how did the whole *discussion* go from getting off your back to getting on mine?"

"I don't know, but why does it matter? It all needed to be said."

Sharon continued picking up napkins and snack bowls as she spoke. "I wanted everything to be right, you know? To have fun together like we used to. I want them to see you like I do—well, short of the fresh-out-of-the-shower sight that sends me into pre-orgasm." She stopped and finally made eye contact. "I wanted it to be right for you. I wanted you to be comfortable, you know?"

"Tonight was too soon, that's all. We have to give them time. We have to give ourselves time."

Laura took the bowls and put them back on the table, then took Sharon's hands and turned her around. "It would all have been said." Fine creases surrounded Sharon's eyes, pressed into concern. "Isn't it better to have it out in the open, to know what everyone is thinking?"

Sharon dropped her gaze. Gently she squeezed Laura's hands. "I guess if there's a deal-breaker there, it's best if I know right now. I was just hopin'—"

"Deal-breaker for what, honey?"

Hesitant eyes returned to Laura's, became direct. "For us."

Laura touched her hand to the side of Sharon's face, cupped the roundness of her cheek. "That's not going to be up to them. Whether or not we make it together is going to be up to us."

Sharon wrapped her arms around Laura, welcomed the reassurance of an embrace. "You don't know how much I want to believe that."

Fingers gently stroked the back of Sharon's head. Laura's mind went to ownership, responsibility. No distractions now. Strong opinions had been silenced, music turned off. Abby had put herself to bed after several unsuccessful round-ups. They were alone.

"It's complicated enough," Laura said, pulling back enough to look into Sharon's eyes. Yes, if you're going to own your feelings and your actions, you should be able to do it looking directly into each other's eyes. "Without letting others tell us what will work and what won't."

"I know they want me to be happy, to be okay. You know? They love me."

"I know they do."

"They stayed by me right through hell."

Laura nodded. "They earned their opinions. I know that. And if I want them to change them, I understand that that has to be earned as well."

Sharon stepped back and took Laura's hand. "You don't have to earn anything. They didn't have to live with me. Don't own more than you have to. There's enough owning up to go around."

"But owning our mistakes is a good beginning, don't you think? Then maybe we can move on to understanding why we made them in the first place."

Sharon nodded, kept Laura's hand and started toward the stairs. "Come on," she said, "I'll clean the rest of this up tomorrow."

"Honey, stop . . . I need us to slow down. I need to talk with you." Sharon's worried look was expected, unavoidable. "Come here, sit down so we can talk."

"It was tonight, wasn't it?" Sharon said as she sat at the card table next to Laura. "It was all too much. I should've known. We won't try that again. We'll just do things, the two of us—and Abbs—okay?"

"We will do things, just us. But tonight I'm going to go back to my mom's. And you and I are going to start doing some serious thinking—alone—without the temptation to let it all ride while we're busy making love."

Where are the distractions when you need them? Even Abby had deserted her. Couldn't they just continue as they were? Pick up the good from before and plug it into place. If only.

"You know I'm crap at analyzing stuff."

"You're not crap at anything—except maybe realizing your own worth. I still remember what you said years ago, before the trial. Do you remember what you told the news reporter at the march?"

She hesitated, not because she didn't remember, but because Laura remembered. "If we don't know our worth . . ."

"How can we expect others to? You have to bring that home, honey. Believe it yourself."

Sharon looked closely at the woman sitting so close, looking so deep. It was the same woman, sending the same sensations tingling through her as when they first met. *Had she told her this before? Why couldn't she remember that?*

"I've never really thought about it—personally, I mean."

"It's important," Laura replied, "for both of us. It's one of the things that I want us to think about, really give serious thought to. We have to know if we feel we are worthy of each other. And that's a lot bigger than it seems on the surface."

"But what if we *don't* feel worthy of the other person? Maybe we feel just lucky."

"How important is this to you?"

The question startled her. "Jesus, Laura, I didn't think you'd have to ask that. You know me. You know that this—that you— are more important than anything to me."

"But I *don't* know that. And I wasn't always the most important thing to you, or you would have gotten help. You would have done what you needed, what I couldn't do for you, to keep us together. And you certainly don't know whether you are the most important thing to me. We don't know who we are right now."

"*That's* what we have to find out? Why didn't you say so? *That* I understand. *That* I can answer."

"No, you can't. Not yet anyway. Because it goes hand in hand with whether we feel worthy of each other. That's why we have to slow down and take whatever time it takes to figure this out. We've both changed, that's to be expected. But, it will take time to find out who we are now."

"You know my heart, and I know yours. That hasn't changed."

"And we found out once already that that wasn't enough. It was enough for love, but not to live together." She reached over and took both of Sharon's hands. "I love you, Sharon. Still. And I know that you love me. I've missed having you in my life more than you know. I've missed your loyalty, and your passion, even your humor." Her brow squeezed into self-questioning. "I'd be somewhere sort of highbrow, getting bored with a stuffy conversation, and I'd start entertaining myself by rephrasing it in my head into Sharon-speak. I couldn't help it, it would just pop into my head and make me smile. I had to excuse myself a couple of times because I was afraid I couldn't hold a giggle down. Even if I wanted to, I don't think I could ever get you totally out of my life . . . So, if we do have a second chance here, I want us to get it right."

Sharon focused on their hands, the physical bond, visible—a faint smile there and gone. "I'm used to working hard," she said, gently squeezing Laura's hands, "physically. Whatever the job is, I know I can do it. Throw any project problem at me and I'll figure it out. It doesn't matter how tired I am, or how much I hurt. I won't let it kick my ass." She brought her eyes back to Laura's. "But this? This scares the hell out of me . . . And I can't just throw a joke out there, and . . . I don't want to mess this up."

"No, we both did a pretty good job of that the first time around, didn't we? But, we can't be afraid to look hard at each other, and be honest about what we expect and what we want. If we don't, we'll be wandering through a maze blindfolded."

"So, you don't think we can figure this out and still spend nights together?"

Laura smiled easily. "How much thinking have you been doing when I stay?"

"At night? None. Not a minute's worth. But, all the next day, I can't stop thinking."

"About why we weren't able to stay together, and what we've learned since?"

"Not exactly." She matched the ease of Laura's smile. "Not at all."

"You know what's so scary about that? It's so much a part of what I love about you . . . and it's exactly why I'm going to stay at Mom's."

Chapter Thirty-Nine

"I think it's the right decision," Deanne said over her shoulder as Sage entered the room.

"To have Cayley spend Sunday with Sharon so that we can have a day to ourselves? Take the convertible out. Sun and wind and country air," she said, wrapping her arms around Deanne's shoulders and speaking softly against her head. "We'll take pictures in the Irish Hills, and stop and eat at some little out of the way place whenever we get hungry."

Deanne bookmarked the page on her screen and leaned into Sage's embrace. She smiled at the tingling warmth—still, forever—wrapped up in a love she hadn't dared dream of. She loved Sage close, deep in thought close, warm breath against her neck. She breathed in the moment and savored it.

Whispered warmth. "Yes?"

"Hey," from the doorway, "Momma Dee."

Deanne offered a quick caress to Sage's cheek. "That's a 'yes,'" she said softly. Then, "What is it, honey?" she replied as Sage stood.

"Can I practice on you? I'm going to teach my class to speak Seneca. Mrs. Andrews said it was okay."

"Sure, honey, that's a great idea." She looked at Sage. "Your idea?"

Sage shook her head. "Cayley's idea—right along with her decision to stay in public school."

"*That's* actually the decision I was talking about when I said that I think it was the right one."

A smile from Sage, private and easy. "I'm trusting you and

Cayley on this one." She planted a kiss on the top of Cayley's head and left the two of them to their lesson.

Trust. The word stood at attention. She'd lost it once, Sage's trust. So now, if it were possible, Deanne thought, she would hold it up high, a flag in a victory lap. Sage's confidence in the substance of someone else's reasoning, her reasoning, meant more than she could say. It would be important enough from most people, but coming from Sage Bristo it was monumental.

Deanne watched Cayley, excited and intent, writing the words neatly on her chalkboard. Children have instincts that we adults have overridden, she'd told Sage. Ask Cayley what she wants. Ask her what she can handle, what she wants to handle. Ask her. And ignore the doubt, when it creeps in now and again, that it was the right thing to do.

"So, what do you think about your new class this year?" she asked, noting a present glint of satisfaction.

"I like it. There's a new girl, she's from Ohio. She likes horses."

"Does Naline like her new school?"

"Yeah. She misses her friends, but I'm sharing mine with her."

Cayley scooted to the edge of her chair and turned the chalkboard around, resting it on her thigh. "Okay," she said with an air much older than her years, "here is your first lesson."

Deanne stifled a smile, and focused on her miniature teacher.

"The Seneca language is called Okwe'owekha' and I am okwe'owe, an Indian." She pointed to the word on the board. "The hardest part is saying the 'o' through your nose," she explained and then repeated its pronunciation.

"It is the hardest part," Deanne agreed and practiced her pronunciation. It wasn't bad, but certainly not anywhere close to her young teacher's proficiency. Her own practice over the years might make the case for genetics. Then again, maybe children have a natural propensity that will allow them to learn easier and faster. "I hope the kids in your class learn faster than I have."

"I'll show them where their tongue goes and then they have to practice like I did."

"What all do you want them to learn in their first lesson?"

Cayley quickly erased the board and wrote the rest of the lesson. "Ike ekeye' he't Okwe'owekha'," she said. "I wish to learn to speak Seneca. And, I'll write everything on the side chalkboard where Mrs. Andrews said we can leave it up until the next lesson."

"You're going to be a very good teacher. And it will be really fun for the class because they will be learning something that no one else in the whole school knows, except Naline."

Cayley nodded enthusiastically. "And Mrs. Andrews wants me to tell them about extinction, too, and the things that Ben taught me. He said that of all the people in the whole world, there are only about a hundred people who can speak Okwe'owekha'. He said they could all fit right in our library room on the reservation. Even Grandma Lena doesn't know how, and she's okwe'owe."

"I'm glad that you like Mrs. Andrews."

"Yeah, she doesn't think Indians are dumb like Mrs. Hanson does."

"I'm not sure that Mrs. Hanson thinks that. Adults sometimes don't hear themselves as children hear them, and they don't always mean what it sounds like."

"No," Cayley said, erasing the board and writing another word, "she thinks we're dumb."

Chapter Forty

The house had been vacant for months. Mortgage payments had tripled, the owners walked, the bank took possession. One more on the already long list of foreclosed properties.

Kasey peered in each window across the width of the front porch, while Sharon went to the back of the house. The living room and dining room were, typically, cluttered with unwanted furniture, and trash bags filled with who knows what. Old carpet in the living room, worn wood floor in the separate dining room. The kitchen wasn't visible, only a narrow doorway leading to it—floor plan circa 1940s.

She left the porch, walked the length of a cracked concrete driveway, and met Sharon in the small backyard. "So, what do you think?"

"Well," Sharon made another passing glance and stopped at a huge tree very close to the attached one-car garage, "that tree is half-dead, already dropped a good-size limb on the roof there. Found a couple of shingles in the side yard, pretty brittle."

"Could you see the kitchen from the side?"

"Window's too high."

Kasey looked around, more closely now at the houses on either side and across the street. "On the up side, it's a solid middle-class neighborhood with a lot of the properties already updated. Might be worth an inspection."

"A dry basement would be—"

Kasey nodded and held up her hand at the ring of her cell phone. She made a quick check. "The realtor," she said, then answered it. "Hi, Arlene. Got some good news for us?" Her eyes met Sharon's, then a smile and a thumbs up. "Yes. Let us know when."

"They took our counter on the Madison Street house?"

"Yep, and the buyers are pre-approved. It's sold," she said with a long-needed high five.

"Well, hell, let's get an inspection on *this* place."

ʒ ʃ ʒ

When a trickle of water starts down a dry riverbed, it makes a thirsty person almost giddy—makes them talk fast, and plan, and forget how tired and sore they are.

Kasey zipped through town, from the realtor's office to basement remodel, mid-mission. "I feel like I've been hunched over under a steel girder for six months," she said, squeezing the truck through an intersection on the yellow light.

Sharon nodded. "Yes, maam, and it feels awful damn good to stand up again."

"Amen."

How does your body do that, Sharon wondered—make your face sort of shine, like Kasey's right now. Not really a smile, but something was lifting her whole face, now bright, childlike, happy.

Kasey glanced quickly to catch Sharon watching.

"This feels good, doesn't it, Kase? Like maybe we're turning a corner. It's just gonna get better now, I can feel it."

"Yes," she replied with a smile, "it's good. We're gonna be okay. We've got rent money coming in and enough remodeling jobs lined up to keep us busy until we get another house."

"I've got a good feeling about the one we just looked at. Even if it's a total tear-down on the roof, if we can get it for under a hundred thousand we're still going to be able to keep the selling price reasonable for the neighborhood."

"I'll crunch the numbers tonight, add in all the worst scenarios and see what Connie thinks we can handle. If not this one, there are plenty out there." She pulled into the drive behind Troy's truck. "Go see how Troy is doing, and I'll call about getting an inspection."

The homeowner was at work, and the basement remodel was finally moving along. The most difficult part of the project was getting the owner to realize that stopgap measures to water-proof a basement almost always come back to haunt you. Once they fail, all that money spent on making that basement functional and fun will be wasted. When that point was under-stood and the leak professionally fixed, the remodel continued in earnest.

Troy had half the suspended ceiling grid in place and greeted Sharon with the end of a T-rail.

"Hey, some great news," she said, holding her end in place. "The Madison Street house sold, and Connie thinks we should pick up another."

"Awesome," he replied. "I know these projects keep us in business, but give me our own house any day. I'd much rather deal with codes than worrying about making a homeowner happy."

"Yeah, and you can play the radio as loud as you want, and swear when you hurt yourself."

"Well, there's that."

"All right," Kasey called, bounding down the stairs, "Morgan's going to squeeze in an inspection next Wednesday. Wow, you're cruisin', Troy."

"One of those days," he said, "rare as they are, when the hammer hits the nail every time."

"Almost makes you forget what you were bitchin' about the day before," Sharon added.

"Okay, let's not interrupt the flow. Come on, Sharon, help me get the ceiling tiles down here."

Flow. They understood flow. Well, maybe not understood, but they appreciated it, courted it almost superstitiously. And ebb. Yes, that, too, they understood, or at least recognized its impact. So, when the day flowed, they squeezed out every last moment of it available, and at its end, they prayed for another.

"If this was a company house," Troy said, putting the last of his tools in the truck, "we'd finish this today before we left."

"That's okay," Kasey replied. "You and I will kick the rest of it out in the morning."

Troy slapped his palm on the fender. "You got it. I told the owner 8:00."

Sharon watched his carefree saunter and waited until she and Kasey were in the truck before asking, "Aren't you and Connie planning on spending the weekend at the cabin? I'll work with Troy tomorrow."

Kasey retrieved a box with a knob and lock set from behind the seat and handed it to Sharon.

"Is this for the basement door?"

"No," Kasey replied, "it goes on the cabin door."

A puzzled look from Sharon.

"Connie and I were thinking that another weekend might be better for us. . . . Do you think you could put this on for me? Maybe you and Laura could take the weekend to get away by yourselves." Puzzled turned to surprised. "There's something magical about that place. Pure and uncomplicated. No distractions or deadlines, no meddling friends." Kasey offered a genuine smile. "Just you and Laura and time for the two of you to find out what you need."

"Thanks, Kasey. This means a lot to me."

"I've been doing a lot of thinking. I've had a tough time finding the boundary, the one even a best friend shouldn't cross. I was assuming it was there, but after all these years, I couldn't tell you where. I don't want to take anything away from what will make you happy. I can't help worrying about you. But I love you, and I need to trust you and just be there if you need me."

"Hey, you're talking to someone who trips over boundaries even when she knows where they are. What matters is knowing that when one of us falls face-first on the wrong side, the other one is there to help us back up. I count on that, Kase."

"Yes, so do I."

"Don't forget to thank Connie for giving up her weekend."

Chapter Forty-One

Over the years the cabin on the lake had been a lot of things; a favorite fishing spot, a gathering place for friends, a quiet retreat. This time, this weekend, it was just as Kasey said it was: magical.

They walked the path around the wooded frontage of the lake, Laura had her hand, Abby was scurrying on and off the path discovering a whole new world of sounds and smells.

"You know what I love most about this place?" Laura asked. "What I *don't* see and hear."

Sharon nodded. "No motors on the lake."

"And no blacktop or concrete, no traffic noise . . . no streetlights at night."

"Yeah, that was freaky for me at first. And I thought it was too quiet. You know, like at night when you can actually hear your heart beating."

Two deep croaks echoed from the water's edge. A dark streak scrambled through the brush. Abby had discovered frogs, big ones. A splash. She discovered that moss-covered rocks are slippery.

More croaks, mocking sounds, accompanying a soaking wet Abby back to the path.

The sound of their laughter mingled with the lake breeze ruffling through poplar leaves, lilting out over the water.

"Come on," Laura said, with a pull on Sharon's hand, "You promised me a boat ride."

Sharon's pull on the oars was steady and smooth. The boat glided through the still water. Laura sat facing Sharon, holding Abby on her lap as the slow, rhythmic movement of the boat took them out past the raft and along the south end of the lake. There didn't seem to be any need for words. They took in the beauty of the lake, the water so clear that they could see the plants swaying from its floor and fish casually swimming in and out of sight. The sun, lower now on the horizon, sent rays sparkling across the surface. Serene. Beautiful.

"Oh, Sharon." Laura turned to realize how far they had traveled. "Honey, turn around, you're going to be so tired."

"My best girls deserve the best boat ride . . . We should probably head back, though. These trees will block the prettiest view of the sunset."

᠕ ᠕ ᠕

They watched the sunset from the boat. tethered at the end of the dock. "I forget how beautiful this is," Sharon said, eyes focused on the huge orange fireball dropping slowing toward the lake. The sky above it began cooling gradually through shades of orange, morphing into a dark pink as the sun dropped completely out of view, leaving the sky layered in dazzling pinks and purples.

"Do you think if we lived in a place like this that we would eventually take this kind of beauty for granted?" Laura asked.

Sharon's gaze remained transfixed on the changing colors. "Like we took each other for granted?"

Laura watched her, so relaxed, at peace. Yes, she loved this woman, in all her many facets. "I wouldn't want that to happen."

Sharon turned. "No, we can't let that happen again."

᠕ ᠕ ᠕

Dinner fulfilled Laura's promise of healthy *and* delicious, with char-grilled salmon and vegetable kabobs. Yes, healthy food can be surprisingly delicious, Sharon was convinced. No convincing was needed for Abby, though, who seemed to devour whatever was set in front of her.

They settled comfortably close to the firepit, Laura on the low log bench, Sharon tending the fire and settling back between Laura's knees. The heat of the burning logs chased away the chill of night air. The smell of the wood was reminiscent and nostalgic, conjuring memories of young friends and innocence and gathering around a crackling fire that centered them in the world. Laura wrapped her arms around Sharon's shoulders. Centered.

"Do you think Abby is sufficiently tuckered?" Sharon asked.

"She's one tired puppy." Abby was stretched on the ground with her belly toward the heat. "I'm betting that she wouldn't object to sleeping by herself in the second bedroom tonight."

"You think?" Sharon said, laying her head back against Laura's chest.

"It's the least she can do." The glow of the fire flickered over Sharon's uplifted face. Laura pressed her own to the warm, soft cheek. "I love you," she said and snugged her arms more tightly.

"If I never heard another word, those three could take me to my grave a happy woman."

"You really mean that, don't you?"

A tilt of Sharon's head found Laura's eyes, their catch lights dancing with the flames. "I do mean it. You know I'm crap at analyzing, seeing anything that doesn't glow in neon right in front of me. But, I finally see it. I finally know that taking care of our love is the most important thing I can do. I just have to learn everything the hard way, I guess."

"Well, that makes two of us." Laura touched her lips lightly to Sharon's. "I didn't know how much I loved my father, or how much I respected my mother. I didn't know that loving you was going to seep into every pore of me, and that I couldn't change that any more than I could change my DNA. But, I know it now." She kissed her deep and long this time, then whispered, "I know it now, honey."

Epilogue

It was a glorious sound, all those voices, men's and women's, their excitement mingled in celebration. The result of Sharon Davis at her social best. They filled the basement of the Community Church, much too large a gathering for anyone's home, and the energy was contagious.

Laura smiled and mingled. She knew many, but not all. There was no doubt, though, that she was back where she belonged. This was her community. Its weaknesses strengthened by numbers, its fears lifted by hope, it would grow and evolve. And she was here to stay, to be a part of it.

Members of the chorus had brought their aluminum platform and assembled it at one end of the basement. Keyboard and speakers and mics were tested with barely a notice, until the choir director took the mic. "Here we go," she said, with the chorus lining up behind her. "Let's sing and dance, and celebrate this day, because we *are* family."

The music and the words, so familiar, so reassuringly true, rang out with conviction. "I got all my sisters and me," Laura sang, squeezing through the crowd looking for Sharon.

But, it wasn't Sharon slipping her arm around Laura's waist and singing in her ear. "Everyone can see that we're together," Kasey sang in that pitch-perfect voice that coaxed Laura to sing louder, to fully engage in the moment. It was a worthy moment.

The crowd moved and sang with the music until its end and then sent up a collective cheer that quieted only when Sharon bound onto the platform.

"Let's celebrate," she said as if the mic wasn't on. "Raise your glasses to all your hard work, and thousands of others across the country, to the one-year anniversary of the signing of the Hate Crimes Prevention Act!"

The erupting cheer was deafening.

Laura watched as an excited Sharon pulled Jenny up the step and embraced her. *Well fought, my love, well fought.*

"You should be very proud of her," Kasey said as the room began to quiet again.

"I am," Laura replied. "And proud that so many people never gave up."

"It's pretty clear that Sharon isn't one to give up easily. She never gave up on you, you know."

"Even I would have called that foolish," Laura replied. "But Sharon's a lot like our community—as strong as she is vulnerable."

"That's our girl," Kasey added with a smile. "And she's at the mic again."

"We have so much more to celebrate tonight. I don't think there is anyone in this room who does not know who Jenny Pearlman Harris is, so I'm just going to give her the mic and the floor and get out of the way. Jenny?"

Clearly not as comfortable being front and center as Sharon was, Jenny smiled through a long applause, then cleared her throat. "I want to thank you all for everything you've done to get this law passed. There is no way that I can even begin to tell you how much it means to me. And I know that a law by itself is not going to stop the hatred, but now that law says that no one has the right to use that hatred to hurt anyone ever again."

There was an air of confidence about her now, Laura noticed. She seemed taller, her voice less hesitant.

"I also want to thank everyone who has helped make the Corbett–Pearlman Scholarship Fund a reality. Every dollar was important. Whether you gave one or one thousand, your contribution has helped create something we can all be very proud of. My mothers opened their home and their hearts to help gay and lesbian teens whose own families had turned their backs on them. To be able to send one of those teens to college every year in their names is an incredible feeling. They would have wanted to be able to pay forward the good in their lives more than anything else they could have asked for—more than remembering their names, more than carrying on without them, even more than fighting to make this bill a law. It has taken me a very long time to understand that. I have concentrated so hard on fighting the hate that I didn't realize how important it is to gather the good. Tonight my mother is surely smiling that *I knew you would finally get it* smile, and Donna is sneaking me that little wink that always lifted me up. So tonight, for them, I have the honor of presenting our first Corbett–Pearlman scholarship to seventeen year-old Tammy Walters from Detroit."

Small in stature, androgynous to the eye, Tammy strode across the platform to take Jenny's hand. But her apparent composure dissolved into a tearful embrace. Whatever she had planned to say, didn't matter. The applause said it for her.

Kasey leaned a shoulder against Laura's. "That sight makes all the effort worthwhile, doesn't it?"

"It does . . . She's the girl whose dad threatened her with a gun, and chased her into the streets. If it hadn't been for the Community Center . . . I can't imagine that kind of fear, not trusting anyone, not knowing where to go to get help."

"Was she afraid to go to the police?"

Laura nodded. "A friend took her to the Community Center, and they contacted the police . . . I'm so glad the committee chose her."

"Congratulations, Tammy," Sharon said, once again at the mic. "We all have a lot to celebrate tonight, and we will. I just have one more announcement to make before we party like I haven't partied in too many years."

Sage wound her way through the crowd toward Laura. If her intent was to warn her, she was too late. She was able only to make eye contact and shake her head as Sharon continued.

"Right now, I am happier than I have ever been. We have a federal law against hate crimes, a much-needed scholarship fund, and the person I love more than my next breath has asked me to marry her."

The result was an eruption of woo-hoos and applause, and a thoroughly embarrassed Laura.

"Sorry," Sage said. "I couldn't stop her."

"Laura, baby," Sharon said, finding her standing near the edge of the room. "I want to spend every day of the rest of my life with you, and I will marry you—the minute Michigan makes it legal."

The chanting began, and Sage draped her arm over Laura's shoulders. "She's off and running."

"I know," Laura replied. "I should have put money on it."

Bywater Books represents the coming of age of lesbian fiction. We're committed to bringing the best of contemporary lesbian writing to a discerning readership. Our editorial team is dedicated to finding and developing outstanding voices who deliver stories you won't want to put down. That's why we sponsor the annual Bywater Prize. We love good books, just like you do.

For more information about Bywater Books and the annual Bywater Prize for Fiction, please visit our website.

www.bywaterbooks.com